TANGLED UP IN PAIN

CHARLOTTE BYRD

Visit my website at www.charlotte-byrd.com

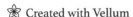 Created with Vellum

Everything comes at a price. What if this one is too high even for him to pay?

Jackson Ludlow, the recluse billionaire of New York, is beautiful and captivating but also damaged and alone.

He thinks he is the only one with secrets, but he's wrong.

My past is coming for me. It's forcing me back there: the place that ruined everything.

I don't want to go. He can't make me.

But there's no way out.

"Fast-paced, dark, addictive, and compelling" - Amazon Reviewer ★★★★★

"Hot, steamy, and a great storyline." - Christine Reese ★★★★★

"My oh my....Charlotte has made me a fan for life." - JJ, Amazon Reviewer ★★★★★

"The tension and chemistry is at five alarm level." - Sharon, Amazon reviewer ★★★★★

"Hot, sexy, intriguing journey of Elli and Mr. Aiden Black. - Robin Langelier ★★★★★

"Wow. Just wow. Charlotte Byrd leaves me speechless and humble... It definitely kept me on the edge of my seat. Once you pick it up, you won't put it down." - Amazon Review ★★★★★

"Sexy, steamy and captivating!" - Charmaine, Amazon Reviewer ★★★★★

" Intrigue, lust, and great characters...what more could you ask for?!" - Dragonfly Lady ★★★★★

DON'T MISS OUT!

Want to be the first to know about my upcoming sales, new releases and exclusive giveaways?

Sign up for my Newsletter and join my Reader Club!

Bonus Points: Follow me on BookBub!

ALSO BY CHARLOTTE BYRD

**All books are available at ALL major retailers! If
you can't find it, please email me at
charlotte@charlotte-byrd.com**

Black Series
Black Edge
Black Rules
Black Bounds
Black Contract
Black Limit

House of York Trilogy
House of York
Crown of York
Throne of York

Standalone Novels

Debt

Offer

Unknown

Dressing Mr. Dalton

CHAPTER 1 - HARLEY

TWILIGHT...

*N*ew York has been my obsession and passion since I was a little girl.

It is easy to fall in love with a city from afar, watching movies and television shows that glorify different aspects of it to suit its own purposes.

Some focus on the dirt and crime, others on wealth.

What they all had in common was change.

New York is the city that can accept the old with the new, where the poor can mingle with the rich, and where everyone has the same opportunities to make their dreams come true.

As any viewer, I was convinced that some of this was, of course, exaggerated for dramatic effect, but that did not stop me from believing the story as a whole.

I came here for its pulsating energy because it's what I thought my life was lacking back home in Montana.

But the truth was that I had underestimated my own interest in that pulsating energy.

I am not someone who will stand outside of a club for hours waiting to get in, wearing four-inch heels, a minidress, and a shawl in the middle of the winter.

I wouldn't even do that in the middle of summer.

That's Julie.

I'd rather make myself a cup of tea and curl up on the couch with a good book.

In fact, before I met Jackson, I'd only been to a handful of parties, most of them back in college and I'd never been to anything as formal as this fundraiser.

The stylist who came to our apartment brought five 'pieces,' her words not mine, for me to try on and a tailor who made adjustments on the fly.

The material was nothing like anything I'd ever felt at a store; it was so light and effervescent.

It felt like powdered sugar in between my fingertips.

And when I looked in the mirror after my hair and makeup was finished, I had never felt so beautiful in my entire life.

Until Jackson looked at me.

His eyes opened wide and his lips parted.

He licked his plump, luscious lower lip slowly as his gaze went up and down my body and then focused on my face.

And now, that dress is laying in a little circle on the floor in the living room, where Jackson took it off me.

I walk over to it, pick it up, and hang it in the closet.

I didn't bring anything else to wear, but luckily the penthouse suite is well stocked with robes and clothes for our use.

Brand new of course.

Just like there are pots, pans, and utensils in the kitchen, the closets are also full of the basics that someone who didn't pack a bag would need.

I put on a pair of black leggings and a loose-fitting long sleeve gray shirt.

Fluffy socks and a pair of slippers complete the outfit and are a nice change from just the sheet, which I had been walking around in ever since I heard the news.

"Talk to me, please," Jackson says, coming out dressed in a dark dressing gown which makes his blue eyes look gray.

His dark hair is tossed and crumpled from our night of passion, but no less gorgeous.

Even in this twilight, his skin isn't sallow, but its usual warm olive color.

"I'm going to make some tea," I say instead.

I go to the large, spotless, white kitchen that looks like it's straight out of a modern living catalog and fill a tea kettle with water from the tap.

When I was a little girl, I loved going through my mother's magazines and making scrapbooks.

You know, cutting out all of these images that struck a chord with me and pasting them into journals.

One was devoted entirely to houses and there was a big section on kitchens that I would have when I grew up.

The appliances are a bit different, but otherwise this kitchen looks exactly like the one I had cut out.

"I'll have a cup."

"What kind do you want?" I ask, going through the wooden box of assorted teas.

"Earl Grey."

"I'll try this Green Tea Mint."

Handing him his cup, we sit down at the dining room table.

I take a sip and let the warm water run down my throat, warming me from the inside out.

Jackson is waiting for me to say something.

Anything.

But no words come.

I'm in shock.

I haven't talked to my father much over the last few years, just an occasional phone call on his birthday and major holidays.

I haven't talked to my mother since we had that fight when I was still in college.

She is as stubborn as I am and so we have just communicated through my dad, even though they are now divorced.

I haven't seen either of them since I left Montana.

And now, suddenly, in the middle of the night, I find out that my mother has been in a car accident and her condition is critical.

My father is begging me to get on the next flight out, but I can't.

"You have to go, Harley. You know that, right?"

"I haven't talked to them in forever. I haven't seen them in a very long time."

"That doesn't matter. Things are different now. If you don't go there and make things right, you will regret it for the rest of your life."

He's right, of course.

Everything he is saying makes sense.

On the surface.

But something is holding me back.

For some reason, I can't bring myself to do it.

"Whatever hesitation you feel right now, it's just fear."

I look up at him. His face is stoic, calm. It's comforting. He isn't freaking out. He's just here...for me.

"I don't think so."

"Are you sure?"

I inhale deeply. I haven't told him much about my life back home.

I haven't told Jackson why I left.

I haven't told Jackson about *him*.

"You don't know anything about this," I say, putting a wall up.

"That's true. So, why don't you fill me in?"

9

CHAPTER 2 - HARLEY

WHEN I BRING MYSELF TO GO...

When I look up at Jackson, our eyes meet and neither of us look away first. We remain locked until I ask, "Why do you even care?"

"You've seen me...without my armor," he says slowly. "You've seen my scars. You felt them. Telling you about that was the hardest thing I've had to do in a long time. If ever."

I nod.

"Now, it's your turn. I want to know you, Harley."

I take a deep breath and launch into my past.

My parents dream of building a ranch that would be their home for generations to come.

The fire that incinerated it and everything along with it.

The trial that resulted in nothing, leaving my parents with nothing.

I save the worst for last.

"I think that my family would've survived the fire though. I mean, we lost everything but if we hadn't lost him, then it would've been different."

"Who?"

"Aspen. My little brother. He was five."

The fire started in the middle of the night when we were all sleeping.

It spread quickly, consuming everything in sight.

The house was full of smoke when I woke up.

Aspen's bedroom was on the other side of the hallway.

We were separated by a wall of fire.

I couldn't get to him.

All I could do was open my window and climb out.

I didn't know if anyone else was going to make it.

I tried going in another way, but there was nothing but fire everywhere.

Then my parents came staggering out.

But Aspen wasn't with them.

They couldn't get to him either.

When the firefighters came, they had to

physically restrain my parents from running back in to get him.

Later we found out that he had died of smoke inhalation long before the flames ever reached him.

So, that was something, I guess.

Tears well up in my eyes.

I've never told that story to anyone before.

My parents tried to make me go to see a therapist, but I refused.

It was easier to just bury it somewhere deep inside of me and never think about it again.

And now, with Jackson, the words just pour out of me.

They come like an avalanche as if they were waiting for this moment all along.

He wraps his arms around me and brings me close.

As I cry, I listen to the beating of his heart.

It thunders in my ears and relaxes me.

I don't know how much time passes as he holds me, but he doesn't push me away not once.

Eventually, no more tears come.

They simply dry up as if there were nothing else in the well.

My parents paid off the house we lived in before

to buy the Burke Ranch, and then my dad forgot to pay one of the insurance payments.

The fire happened soon after and the insurance company used that as an excuse to deny their claim.

They took the matter to trial but lost the case.

"After losing Aspen and all of their retirement savings, they

couldn't deal with life anymore. I found my mother texting with an old high school boyfriend and she was having an affair with him. She and I had a huge fight and we never spoke again. They eventually divorced but stayed on somewhat amicable terms, I guess, since they still talked."

Jackson nods and takes another sip of his tea.

"Do you really think I need to go back?"

He nods.

"But what if everything turns out fine? I mean, she could just get better."

"What if she doesn't?"

I shake my head.

"Look, I know that you don't want to go home, especially given how bad the situation is. But if you don't go back for your mom, then you have to go back for your dad. He's all alone there in that hospital room. He needs your support."

I shake my head and take another deep breath.

He's right.

Of course, he's right.

Finally, I grab my phone and start searching for flights.

Of course, there are no direct flights and I'm lucky to find one with only one stop rather than two.

It costs almost a thousand dollars.

Shit.

I shake my head.

"What are you doing?"

"Looking for flights."

"So, you're going?" he asks, a little smile forming at the corner of his lips.

"Yes, I am." I roll my eyes in exasperation. "Even though it's going to cost like a grand to leave tonight and I have a four hour layover in Chicago."

He stares at me with a dumbfounded expression on his face.

"Is that what you were doing? Looking for flights?"

"Um, yes, what else?"

"Why don't you just take my plane?"

WHILE JACKSON IS on the phone making

arrangements, I stare out of the window, which begins at my feet and stretches above my head, at the gray skyline.

Apparently, Earnest Hemingway once asked F. Scott Fitzgerald what makes the rich different from the rest of us. Fitzgerald stared at him and then answered, "They have more money."

That's one of those quotes that always made me laugh a little to myself.

What I didn't realize was how wise it really was until this moment.

As someone without money, I would've had to spend half of my measly monthly paycheck on a ridiculously long flight to get home.

And what does Jackson have to do?

Just make a phone call and order his plane.

I don't know yet, but I bet it will be a direct flight.

A part of me wants to say no out of principle.

I am an independent woman who pays her own bills and she likes it that way.

But I don't really want to go home in the first place and that makes paying for a crammed flight through O'Hare airport in Chicago a lot less appealing.

"Okay, it's all set up. The pilot will be there in an hour."

"Oh, I don't think that's enough time. I have to go home and pack."

"That's okay, he'll wait. He won't leave without you."

I stare at him, trying to process what he has just said. The plane will wait for me? *Me*?

"Yes, the plane will wait for you," Jackson says, reading my mind.

CHAPTER 3 - HARLEY

WHEN WE GO...

"Mr. Garbo will drop me off and then come back to take you to the airport," Jackson says when we pull up to Julie's apartment dressed in our penthouse-issued clothes.

"It shouldn't take me long to pack if you wait and then I can come with you while you pack," I suggest.

"What do you mean?" he asks.

I stare at him.

"Wait, you want me to come with you?"

It never even occurred to me that he wouldn't.

I mean, I didn't think he would when I was looking up flights to go commercial.

But I am taking his plane.

"I thought that since you were offering your plane that I would...you would...come with me."

"It's really not a big deal. It's just like being on a regular plane; it's just all yours and it goes to a different airport. You'll be fine."

I don't know if he is being dense on purpose or he is just obtuse. So, I just come out and say it.

"Can you come with me?"

The words come out soft and shy.

But his response is quick and confident.

"Of course."

PACKING DOESN'T TAKE THAT LONG on either of our parts and we are pulling up to the airport in no time.

I've never been anywhere like this before. Instead of parking and dragging our bags through the main entrance, waiting for them to get checked, and then going through the long process of security, here Mr. Garbo just pulls up to one of the sparkling white planes on the tarmac and gets our bags out of the trunk.

I go to get mine, but Jackson stops me.

"They'll take care of them for us."

I grab my purse and follow him up the stairs leading right into the plane. Inside, a flight attendant welcomes us inside and shows me to one of the

spacious leather seats near the center of the plane.
It's about as big as a recliner that my father used
to have.

To the left of me, are another two seats facing
each other with a desk in the middle.

Unlike regular planes, where all the seats are
facing the front, this one is arranged like a living
room.

Jackson sits down in the large recliner across
from me.

The flight attendant asks us if we would like
anything.

Suddenly, feeling drained from all the emotions
of the night, I ask for a coffee.

"Two coffees, please," Jackson says.

"Would you like anything to eat?" the flight
attendant asks.

"What do you have?"

"Croissants, bagels, cereal, lox. I can also make
you some eggs, any way you want."

"I'll take a croissant."

"What kind?"

"What kind do you have?"

"Plain, chocolate, hazelnut, oatmeal."

"Hazelnut, I guess."

When he walks away, I turn to Jackson and joke

that was way too many decisions to make so early in the morning.

Soon after we are served breakfast, the plane takes off.

We pierce through the cloud cover in no time and find ourselves in the bright blue sky above.

"This is…beautiful."

"I'm glad you like it."

"So, this is your plane?"

"Yes. I haven't used it in a long time though, so I leased it out."

I nod as if that makes perfect sense.

People lease planes?

Is it like leasing cars?

Jackson sits back in his recliner, relaxing.

He is wearing a suit, but a less formal one than I saw him in before.

There's no tie.

The shirt is starched and ironed, but the top button is left open.

His dress shoes are polished, giving them a bright shine.

My gaze falls to the floor, which I notice is carpeted in a thick expensive weave.

"How's your croissant?"

"Delicious. I've never had a hazelnut croissant before."

"Neither have I," Jackson responds.

"Here, have some," I volunteer.

He shakes his head, staring right at me.

"Only if you come over and feed it to me," he says with a smile.

His smile is contagious.

I can't help but smile, too.

I get out of my seat and walk over to him.

Sitting down on the arm of his chair, I carefully bring the croissant to him.

He opens his mouth and takes one large sensual bite.

"Mmm, that is good."

"Told you." I get up to leave, but he pulls me back toward him.

"Where are you going?"

"What? You want more? You asked for a bite. You can't have more."

"Oh, yes, I can." He reaches for me and grabs the croissant out of my hand, taking another big bite.

Laughing and wrestling, we break the croissant into pieces and watch with disappointment as it crumbles in our hands.

Suddenly, Jackson reaches over and kisses me.

His lips are soft at first, but then they become more needy.

More demanding.

I lose myself in his mouth.

In that moment, the world outside disappears and nothing else exists except the two of us.

A few moments later, I pull away and look at him.

"Is everything okay?"

"It is now that you're kissing me."

"I can do more than kiss."

I smile. "I wish, but we can't do it here, right?"

I can't see the flight attendant behind the curtain, but I know he's there.

Jackson shakes his head. "This is my plane. If we need privacy, we will have privacy."

I furrow my brow, not entirely sure where he's going with this.

He reaches over to the panel of buttons on his chair and presses the one with the word 'PRIVATE' on it.

"What does that do?"

"Now, the flight attendant will know not to bother us."

"Under what circumstances."

"Under no circumstances. He will not come back here until I press that button again."

"But what if there's some sort of emergency?" I ask, not really believing him.

"I'm not a pilot. If there's an emergency, then he'll have to turn to her. Besides, if we do nosedive, I'm pretty sure we'll know."

"I did not need that image in my head," I point out.

"Let's play a game to take your mind off things?" he asks. "You do everything I say, no matter what it is."

CHAPTER 4 - HARLEY

WHEN WE PLAY A GAME...

When he makes that request, his voice gets lower and more authoritative, sending shivers down my back.

But I'm not afraid, I'm excited.

I press my toes into my shoes and my heels lift off a bit from the floor.

Jackson sits up a bit in his chair and unbuttons the middle button of his suit.

I bite my lower lip, remembering how good his butt felt in my hands.

"Take off your shoes."

I unzip my ankle boots and step out of them.

"Socks."

I pull them off and place them in the boots.

Jackson's eyes run over my body until they find

the precise thing they want to focus on.

"Pants."

I unbutton the top of my jeans and pull down the zipper. Then I slowly pull them over my butt the way I've seen women do in movies.

"Turn toward me."

My heart skips a beat.

I've never been bossed around and I never thought that I would like it.

But I do. I really do.

It's hard to explain how excited it makes me to do as he says.

I turn my body toward him.

My moves are a lot less smooth, but he doesn't laugh, so that's enough, I guess.

When I get them down to my knees, I trip and nearly fall to the floor, but catch myself at the last moment.

"I'm sorry, I've never done this before."

"Take off your jeans?"

His smooth voice gives me a hot flash.

Instead of a sweet man who comforted me when I first learned about my mom's condition, he is suddenly ruthless and hard.

Unforgiving.

Perfect and cold like a marble statue.

And this is the man who made my blood run warm and my whole body burn for him.

When I toss my jeans on the ever-growing pile of clothes, I turn to him.

Now, all that remains is a light blue cardigan, a pink blouse, and a matching set of bra and panties.

Both in white.

"Take off your sweater," Jackson says next.

His dark eyebrows perfectly frame his piercing blue eyes with thick envious lashes.

My eyes light up as I look at his sculpted cheekbones and down at his luscious lips full of wicked words.

"Blouse, too."

A moment later, I'm standing before him in nothing but my bra and panties.

Again, he tells me to turn around, slowly.

"Why?"

"I want to look at every part of you."

I take a deep breath.

The perfect body of a Victoria's Angel, I do not have.

But it is what it is, and I have slowly grown to accept it.

Yes, I still wish that my thighs didn't touch when I walked or that my breasts were a little bigger to make up for how wide my waist is, but I can't change any of those things anytime soon.

"You are...stunning."

I turn around to face him and see how mesmerized he is by me.

It's as if he sees none of the faults.

He looks at me and he sees someone beautiful.

It practically takes my breath away.

"Come here," he says in his smooth, mesmerizing voice.

I do as he says and he puts me on his lap, spreading my legs around his as I climb into his seat with him.

He uses his hands to unclasp my bra and lets my breasts fall before him.

He watches them bounce before leaning over and taking one in his hand and the other in his mouth.

I lean my head back in pleasure.

His kisses are greedy as he is about to devour me.

He holds the small of my back tightly without letting go.

When he finally pulls away, the warmth that was building up inside of me drenches my underwear.

Jackson moves his hand down my body and buries it inside of me.

He pushes his fingers deep inside and my legs spread wider to accommodate him.

My body responds instinctively toward his, making it impossible for me to contain my arousal anymore.

I reach for him, but he pushes my arms away.

"Take off your underwear."

Without moving my body much, I do as he says, yearning for him in anticipation.

"Now, put your hands on my knees and open wide."

As much as I want to touch him, I do as he says.

I prop myself up by holding onto his knees and giving him space to pleasure me.

He takes a moment to spread me out wide and look at every part of me.

Whatever embarrassment I felt has vanished completely and is surpassed by my overwhelming feeling of arousal.

I need him.

I crave him.

I want him to take me over that edge.

When I clench my legs together, he pushes them apart.

Pushing his fingers deep inside of me he starts

moving them in and out, slowly speeding up his rhythm.

I hang my head back and lose myself in the moment.

But just as I am getting close to that explosion I demand, he pulls out.

After unbuckling his pants, he slides them down.

He slides on a condom and plunges his large cock inside of me, piercing my body almost in two.

Suddenly, our movements become fluid.

We move as one wave.

Slow at first.

Then faster and faster.

The familiar warm feeling starts to overwhelm me.

But this time, it builds fast.

So fast that I don't even see it coming until I'm moaning his name in his ear.

"Harley," he groans in response before lowering me on top of him.

CHAPTER 5 - JACKSON

AFTER...

*a*s she lays naked on top of me, drenched in sweat, I want her again.

But my body is spent and it will take some time to recover my strength again.

Whatever trepidations I had about accompanying her to Montana have all vanished.

After Harley pulls herself off me, she gets dressed and I clean myself up and pull up my pants.

She takes her seat across from me and takes another sip of her coffee.

"Thank you for that," she says.

"And, thank you."

She laughs a quiet little laugh and shakes her head.

"No, I mean, for all of this. For the distraction."

"Oh, is that all I am?" I joke. Her smile vanishes and her face gets a grave expression.

"No...you are so much...more than that."

"Good, because you are, too."

I don't press the privacy button again until we are both presentable. When the flight attendant comes over, I ask for a bottle of water and Harley asks if he has any candy.

"Yes, what kind of candy are you looking for?"

"M&M's? They're my favorite."

"Plain or peanut."

"Plain."

When he comes back with a king-size pack, Harley climbs onto her chair with both feet and wraps her arms around her knees.

Then she makes a delicate rip in the side of the bag, fishes around in there, and pulls out a yellow one.

"They always say that they taste the same, but yellow ones are my favorite."

I smile.

"Do you want one?"

I shake my head. "I'm not a big fan of chocolate."

She stares me as if she has just seen a three headed dragon and adds, "More for me then."

We don't talk much after that.

She pulls out her headphones and loses herself in the music on her phone.

Eventually, she reclines her chair and falls asleep.

I get a blanket from the side bin and cover her up with it.

High above the clouds, the reality of everyday life seems far away. Perhaps it's the distance from the ground or, I tend to think, it's the movement.

I don't know how fast this plane is flying, but it feels like it's fast enough to take us away from all of our problems.

But then again, there's the issue of landing.

Once you descend and the wheels touch the earth again, you're grounded in another place with its own problems.

Never in a million years did I think that someone like Harley would crash into my life and bring me out of the spell under which I lived, no, existed.

It was like I had spent four years in the dark and now I could see the light, breathe the air, and smell the flowers.

I wasn't sure if she would take me up on my offer of a plane, and I was surprised by her invitation for me to come.

But now that we're going, meeting her family seems like the most natural thing in the world.

After being cooped up in my house for so long, I yearn to see what the world has to offer. I never traveled much.

Before I got money, I never had money and always worked to make it. Instead of backpacking through Europe or Asia like some of my friends from college, I worked.

I was what they now call a serial entrepreneur.

I tried this idea and that idea.

I tried to sell secondhand goods on my website and I tried investing in a $10,000 house in a bad part of Philadelphia and flipping it.

My investment was only a grand, but I did make out with four in the end, so that was...something.

In addition to these ideas, there were also many more that never resulted in anything.

But I kept trying.

I think that was the key to my success.

Just doing until...

Trying until I was successful.

Now, looking back, I wonder where I got that courage to keep going in the face of all that failure.

But I did and I'm happy for that.

What's ironic is that the blog that I started that

eventually became the Minetta Media Co. wasn't started as some money-making scheme.

It was just a place for me to write about my ideas and thoughts.

Fortunately, I didn't have a job at the time and I needed to monetize it and, well, the rest is history.

High above the clouds, you only get glimpses of the earth below, but it is still noticeable how quickly farmland below becomes wide open plains for miles and miles.

I've never been to Montana, but I've seen the movies and I've read a few books in which it plays a major role.

I wonder if it is as beautiful as they say.

As soon the plane starts to descend, I know that it is.

Rolling hills of wilderness below fill my window.

When we get closer, I see that the hills are filled up with trees, and if I can see them from here, they must be tall.

A narrow river winds through the wilds and a few lakes dot the land. Harley doesn't stir until the wheels collide with the ground.

"Are we here?"

I nod, pulling myself from one beautiful sight to

look at another. This woman who welcomed me into her life and rescued me.

She looks out of the window. "Yep, that's Missoula," she says.

The sky is gray and flurries are twirling outside the window.

We exit the plane, clutching our coats tight around our necks, and walk directly into the waiting town car.

The driver loads our baggage into the trunk.

The airport isn't much to look at, but most airports aren't.

But then, when we drive away from it and into the hills around it, I am taken aback by the height of the trees and thickness of the woods.

"It's beautiful here," I say.

Harley nods, looking out of the window.

"Yes, it is."

"Is this how you remember it?"

"Pretty much. Maybe with a bit more snow."

Harley wants to go to a hotel to drop our stuff off, but I suggest we go straight to the hospital.

"We can always drop it off later," I say. "He'll wait."

"I don't want him to wait," she says sternly.

"It's no problem, ma'am," the driver pipes in.

35

I get the feeling that Harley is just trying to buy time.

She's not ready to see her mom or her dad but going to a hotel first isn't going to solve anything.

"We'll do whatever you want," I finally say.

It's her family and she does know them best.

She shakes her head. "I don't think I can do this, Jackson. I mean, I haven't seen them in...so long."

The car pulls up to the curb by the hospital's entrance. I get out, but Harley doesn't. I open her door.

"You can do this. I'm here for you."

CHAPTER 6 - HARLEY

WHEN WE GET THERE...

y whole body is trembling when I finally climb out of the town car.

I take Jackson's strong hand and let him lead me inside.

The person at the front desk asks for our identification and then takes our pictures for our visitor pass stickers.

"Please keep these on at all times," he instructs.

"Can you tell us where we can find Lounge Area B?" Jackson asks.

The guard shows us on a map and points us in the right direction.

"Why is he asking me to meet him there? Why can't I go straight to her room?" I ask Jackson, referencing the text that I received from my dad while we were driving.

He shrugs, not knowing much more than I do about what's going on.

When we get to the lounge area, we walk through the open double doors and enter a large space with tables and chairs that resembles a cafeteria.

In the corners, there are soft pieces of furniture, the same maroon color that all hospital furniture seems to be.

There are a few people making themselves comfortable by spreading out on a few chairs at once and watching the television screens which are all turned down low.

I see the back of my father's head in the cluster of couches on the other side of the room.

There's someone else with him.

I don't know who they are because they're all facing away from me.

Their heads bob as we approach, buried deep in conversation.

"Dad?" I ask when we are within earshot.

My father gets up immediately and throws his arms around me.

He sobs into my shoulder and I burst out in tears as well.

My father rarely cries.

One of the only times that I can remember was at Aspen's funeral.

We hold each for awhile and just cry.

Then when I try to pull away, he whispers into my ear.

"I'm so sorry, Harley. This wasn't my idea. Please believe me."

His words come all at once and he shakes me a bit as he talks.

None of them really register until he finally lets me go.

"Harley—"

I can't see her face through the tears, which are still flowing as if the dam has recently been broken, but I recognize her voice immediately.

No, it can't be.

What is going on?

I wipe my eyes and look at the woman standing before me.

My mother.

Unscathed and perfectly fine.

"Are you feeling better?" I ask, at a loss as to how

39

and why she can be so normal looking given what my father told me happened. "You shouldn't be standing."

"Harley," she says in her stern police officer voice.

My body reacts just like it did when I was little and heard that policewoman tone. I stand up straight, with my chin up and my chest up.

"Mom...what's going on?"

Before my mom says a word, a stranger walks up to me and puts her arms around my shoulders.

She introduces herself as Dr. Esther Low.

"Dad, what is going on here?" I demand to know, and I pull myself away from this woman who is trying to calm me down.

Both of my parents look at Dr. Low who asks me to sit down in the chair.

I ignore her. "So, you're...better then?"

My words are thin and grasping.

It feels like deep down inside I know the truth, but I can't admit it to myself.

She was in a car accident and now she's fine.

It's a miracle, I say to myself.

That's all it is.

"Please sit down, Harley," Dr. Low says, leading me to one of the chairs with the worn light wooden handles, which too many people have held onto when they heard bad news.

I sit down and Jackson sits next to me.

My parents sit to the right and left of us, completing an imaginary circle.

Being a little bit more aware of my senses, I look at them.

My father is cowering in his seat, looking...guilty?

But guilty of what?

My mother, on the other hand, is sitting straight up, assuming her best cop posture.

There isn't a scrape on her face and her hair has recently been cut and colored.

Even her makeup, which she always wears, is perfect.

"Harley, your mother has tried to reach out to you a number of times and you have always refused to answer, is that correct?" Dr. Low says.

"I don't understand what's going on here. Mom?"

"Please answer her question, Harley."

I look at Jackson and then my dad and then back to Dr. Low.

"Yes, we had a fight. She called a few times; I was mad so I didn't answer."

"And according to your mother, you have cut off

41

communications a long time ago and haven't spoken since."

"She knows why."

"Her mother has come to terms with her mistakes."

This makes me so angry, my blood starts boiling.

I jump out of my seat and then turn around and address her and only her.

"Were you or were you not in a car accident?"

She doesn't reply.

"Because it doesn't look like it, Mom. It doesn't look like it one bit. But the thing is that sitting here with this woman, I'm starting to think that you just made this whole thing up to get me to come here."

My whole body is shaking again.

Cold sweat is running down my back.

My hands are frozen, and I can't feel a single finger.

Now, all of my tears have dried.

It's as if they were incinerated by the anger that's building in the pit of my stomach.

"Please tell me that's not what you did, Mom. Please! I beg you."

Finally, my mom's stern demeanor develops a crack in it.

She slouches a bit in her chair and looks away from me, unable to meet my gaze.

"I'm sorry," she finally whispers.

CHAPTER 7 - HARLEY

WHEN IT FADES TO BLACK...

*E*verything else that comes after that is a blur.

Dr. Low tries to talk to me.

She doesn't dare put her arm around me again or even touch me, but she approaches me and tries to explain.

I don't know exactly what her job is here, but she reminds me of one of those people who run interventions on cable television.

The only problem is that I don't have a problem.

I'm not an addict and I don't need saving.

My mom does.

"I just wanted to bring you here and talk to you. I wanted you to give me a chance," my mom pleads.

"So, you lied about being in critical condition.

44

You made me worry? You made me interrupt my life and hop on a plane and come here to what, talk to you about the past? Didn't you think that I would have a few things to say about the present?"

"That's why we brought Dr. Low."

"Oh, yeah?" I turn to the doctor. "Is this what you do? Do you specialize in making up car accidents or is this just one of your many areas of expertise? How about death? You ever make up a murder?"

"Please, Harley, you are blowing this out of proportion," my mom insists.

I take a step toward her, my face is so close to hers that I can hear the shallowness of her breaths.

"You lied to me, Mom. You made me worry. You made me come here under false pretenses. I'm never going to forgive you for this."

I don't wait for her answer. I just turn around and walk toward the door. Jackson follows quickly behind me.

When we get outside, a gust of fresh air hits me by surprise.

My coat was draped on my forearm, but I quickly put it on and zip it all the way up.

When Jackson walks up to me, I turn to face the wind and enjoy the way it hits against my face.

It's probably close to ten degrees with the wind chill, but the tingles against my cheeks feel good.

It's a good kind of pain, unlike the one that I left behind in that hospital lounge.

Instead of saying anything to me, Jackson just puts his arms around me and squeezes tightly.

We stand here silently for a few moments until my thoughts can't be contained anymore.

"How could she do this to me?" I ask. "How could she just lie like that? And why did he go along with it?"

Jackson doesn't have the answers to these questions anymore than I do. But he stands there holding me until I get too cold and that's enough.

"Can we get back to the car?" I ask, with my teeth chattering.

He laughs.

"I thought that you would never ask."

The driver is waiting for us in the parking lot. The car is toasty and warm, and Jackson tells him that we're just going to sit here for a few minutes.

"No, I want to go," I insist.

"Where?"

"Home."

"You want to fly all the way there, now?"

I nod.

"Aren't you tired?"

"Of course, I'm tired. But that doesn't mean that I want to spend anymore time here than absolutely necessary."

"I rented us a cabin not far from here. About a ten-minute drive."

"A cabin?"

He shrugs. "I've never been here before so I thought I'd rent something mountain-themed."

I look out of the window.

I'm too tired and emotionally exhausted to be in the position to make any decisions.

All I want to do is to lie down somewhere, close my eyes, and make the world go away for awhile.

Jackson takes that as a yes and ten minutes later I am walking up the stairs of a large A-frame mountain chalet.

We walk through the enormous double doors and are welcomed by a grand fireplace, the kind they have in medieval castles.

The great room is spacious with towering ceilings and windows that go all the way to the top from the floor.

The view from the great room is onto a large meadow which disappears into the darkness.

The part that I do see is covered in virgin snow and a few animal tracks.

"This is a cabin?"

Jackson shrugs. "It's all that was available."

"In Missoula? I find that hard to believe," I joke.

"Don't worry about it. It's my treat."

"It better be, because I can't afford this place."

Jackson carries my suitcase to the enormous master bedroom upstairs with its own fireplace. I climb up on the king-size four-poster bed and curl up on one side.

"I'm so sorry that they did that to you," Jackson says. "That was...really shitty."

I don't really know what to say.

I don't want to summon the anger that is simmering just under the surface.

I want to keep it at bay.

Keep it away from this beautiful place.

But I can't.

Every thought I have is about her and what she did.

"What kind of person does something like that to someone they love? I mean, to lie to me like that? I mean, what was she thinking?"

"Maybe she was just desperate."

I practically growl at him.

"I'm not taking her side. I'm just trying to come up with possibilities."

"She's a sociopath. How about that for a possibility? An egomaniacal psychopath."

Jackson nods. "When was the last time you spoke to her?"

I shrug. "I can't remember."

"When was the last time she reached out to you?"

"A few weeks ago."

"And before that?"

"About six months ago. Why?"

"Just trying to understand where she was coming from."

"Nowhere good. If she wanted to see me so badly, why didn't she just hop on a plane herself? She could've just showed up at my door. I wouldn't have turned her away."

He doesn't say anything in reply. I've had enough for one day. I lie back down on the pillow and close my eyes.

"I'm just going to...relax...for a bit," I whisper and slowly drift away.

CHAPTER 8 - HARLEY

WHEN SNOW FALLS...

*I*t takes me a moment to realize where I am when I wake up.

The sun is high in the sky and shining brightly through the windows.

The light that's streaming in is cheerful and for a moment I enjoy it, but then all the memories of what just happened come flooding in.

My mother lied about being in a car accident.

She orchestrated this whole ruse just to bring me out to talk to her about our problems.

Did she really think that bringing me here under false pretenses would improve our relationship?

I climb out of bed and stretch my arms high above my body.

I had forgotten how absolutely clean and aromatic the air is here.

Even though it's winter, and nothing is blooming, the air is still different somehow than it is in New York.

Away from pollution and people, it's easier to breathe.

It's like there's more oxygen here.

I inhale three times for good measure, trying to hold onto this feeling.

Walking downstairs, I expect to see Jackson sprawled out on the couch or perhaps working on his laptop on the kitchen island, but he's nowhere to be found.

There are more rooms upstairs and I regret not calling his name until I got here.

Instead of walking all the way back up, I yell his name at the top of my lungs, hoping that my calls will reach every corner of this gigantic manor.

No one responds.

I call again.

Again no one responds.

When I walk up to the fridge, I see a note attached to it with a magnet.

. . .

I'LL BE BACK *in a bit.*

Love,

Jackson

LOVE.

Why did he write love here?

Is he just being polite?

Or does this actually mean what it says?

My mind starts to wander in circles.

He has never said those three magical words to me before and I have never said them to him.

Is this an inkling of how he really feels?

Stop this.

Stop this immediately, I say to myself.

You have enough to worry about.

Just take the note at face value and that's it.

Unsure of where Jackson went or when he'll be back, I decide to venture outside. I'm not a big fan of the cold, but I would be lying if I said that I didn't miss the cold the way it in in Montana.

In the Rockies, there's hardly any humidity and the dryness gives the air a crispness that doesn't exist back east.

Every day feels entirely new, fresh, never touched.

Never marred.

I put on my winter gear and step outside.

I run around to the back of the house toward the beautiful meadow surrounded on all sides by thick forests of towering pines.

The snow makes a loud crinkling sound under my boots.

I sweep my mitten in it and it falls apart like powdered sugar.

There isn't a wet flake here.

When I close my eyes, I see him again.

He always hated wearing hats and my parents virtually insisted on them, but he would take them off immediately as soon as he was out of sight.

One of our favorite things to do together was to plop down in the snow and make snow angels.

I lean back and let myself go.

My body falls limp into a thick pile of snow, right above a little grove.

Its softness brings me in and cushions my fall.

I lie here for a moment before opening my eyes. He is laughing and smiling and calling my name to do it again and again.

I want to hold onto this feeling as long as I can because once I open my eyes, it will be gone.

But he disappears as quickly as he appeared, before I even have the chance to pull away first.

Slowly, I open my eyes and look at the bright blue sky. Yesterday's gray has been supplanted by today's blue.

There isn't a cloud in the sky and the sun beaming down on me makes me actually feel hot.

I pull my arms through the parting snow from my thighs all the way to the top of my head and down again.

Almost involuntarily, my legs follow.

They separate and spread out evenly over the snow.

Now, comes the hardest part.

If you want your snow angel to be perfect, and you do, you have to get up in such a way as to not disturb it.

Even though my face feels warm, my butt is starting to go numb and I know that it's time to get up.

Bringing my legs back together, I sit up and carefully try to get up without using my hands for support.

Unfortunately, given everything that I'm wearing, that task is practically impossible.

So, instead, I place my hands behind my back and nudge myself forward.

When I'm on my feet, I jump as far away as possible so as not to leave any shoe prints around the snow angel and reveal its true identity.

I jump pretty far and when I turn around to take a look at my handiwork, my eyes tear up.

This is the kind of snow angel that would make Aspen proud.

I stand here looking at it and waiting.

Waiting for what exactly?

I don't know.

A sign perhaps.

A sign that he is not gone forever.

That he is still here...with me.

A gust of wind comes and swirls around me.

It's so strong that it picks my hat off my head and tosses it into snow. It takes me a few gallops to catch up to it.

Was that it?

Was that what I was waiting for?

Or was that just the wind?

I head back inside without a clear answer.

CHAPTER 9 - HARLEY

INSIDE...

*J*ackson is still not back, so I make myself a cup of tea and open my journal.

I don't even know where to start now.

So much has happened. I don't want to write about my mother. That's too painful, too recent.

So, my thoughts turn to fiction.

It's always easier to lose yourself in versions of the truth rather than in the truth itself.

I read through what I have already: sketches of a man much like Jackson.

But where is this story going?

What does he want?

What does he need?

A woman.

She will be like me, but not exactly like me.

A version of me.

I begin a new chapter from her perspective.

She's new to New York and she loves every part of it.

I try to continue, but out here among acres of wilderness, New York seems like something I made up in a feverish dream.

No, I have to write about something more real.

Yes, of course.

The woman will meet the man.

She will beat down his door and beg for his help.

Shivers run down my spine as I relive what happened.

But in my writing, it's a bit different.

A bit skewed.

Electrified.

But then I stop mid-sentence.

It's too much.

The memories flood my mind and mix in with the memories of yesterday and of Aspen, and it's all too much.

I can't write.

Not about this.

Not yet.

"Hey!" Jackson walks in through the door, holding a box from the Missoula Bakery.

He flips it open, facing me and my mouth immediately starts to water for the yummy goodies inside.

"Aren't you even going to give me a kiss first?" he asks as my fingers reach for the eclair.

I grab it and give him a passionate kiss on the lips.

"You are...amazing," I mumble, taking a bite of the treat. He shakes his head.

"Wow, I had no idea you were such a fan of baked goods. I would've gotten you some sooner."

"First of all, who isn't a fan of baked goods? And secondly, yes, you should have. Totally should have. And the fact that you haven't is something that I will hold against you forever."

He grabs a plain croissant and pours himself a cup of coffee from the pot he made earlier.

"You're not a big fan of coffee, are you?" he asks.

I shake my head.

"I'll have it once in a while, but I'm a tea kind of girl."

I don't know why I'm suddenly in such a good mood.

Maybe it's just seeing him again.

Or maybe it's because he brought me the most delicious eclair in the world.

"When did you wake up?"

"Not long ago."

"Seriously?"

I nod. "Why did you let me sleep so late?"

"You were really exhausted last night. And after everything that happened, you needed to rest."

"Well...I appreciate it. Thank you."

He nods.

While we eat, it slowly dawns on me that something is different. He isn't exactly the same.

There's an eagerness to him that I haven't seen before.

It's like he's trying to influence me in some way or to get me to do something.

"Is everything okay?"

"Yes, of course," he says a little too fast.

I narrow my eyes.

He's lying to me.

And he's not very good at it.

What's going on here?

"Tell me what's going on," I demand to know.

"Nothing...nothing bad," he stumbles over his words.

The confidence and the self-assuredness that I

came to believe he embodied at all times is suddenly gone.

Vanished.

"Please don't lie to me, Jackson. I can't handle anymore lies right now."

He nods and looks away. His eyes won't meet mine. My stomach begins to rumble. I'm not hungry, but I am anxious. My palms get sweaty. What did he do?

"Okay," he says, taking a deep breath. "Promise me you won't get mad."

"That's impossible since I have no idea what you are about to say."

"So, promise anyway."

I shake my head.

"Don't play games, Jackson. I don't like games."

He takes a deep breath.

"Will you at least promise to hear me out?"

I think about that for a moment and then give him a nod.

"I met with your father this morning."

I drop my half-eaten eclair onto the floor.

When it collides, it bounces up and the filling explodes out of it, covering my feet and legs in delicious sweet sugary cream.

CHAPTER 10 - HARLEY

WHEN I DON'T HEAR HIM...

"Wait, a second, what do you mean you met with my father this morning?" I say the words, but they don't make anymore sense coming out of my mouth than they do from his.

Jackson takes a few steps away from me.

I come forward.

"Listen, I don't want you to get upset—" he starts to say, but I cut him off.

"Why the hell were you meeting with my father behind my back?"

"He called me."

"How did he even get your number?"

We are getting off track, I don't really care.

What I care about is why he went there.

I mean, of course, I know why.

My father is trying to make nice on my mother's behalf, like he always does.

That has been his job ever since I was a little girl.

My mom makes a mess, and my father cleans it up.

Kind of ironic, since she's a cop and all.

"I'm not sure, but he mentioned Julie."

I shake my head. "Of course. I gave her your number just in case. Not for her to give out to just anybody."

"Your father isn't just anybody."

My body is fuming.

I feel so betrayed.

How could he meet with him?

It's like what they did to me last night doesn't matter.

Whatever means possible to justify the ends, right?

I walk away from Jackson and pace around the room.

I am torn between never wanting to speak to him again and needing him to tell me what they talked about.

"I'm sorry that I met with him, Harley. What else can I say?"

"Are you sorry because it was the wrong thing to do?"

He takes a deep breath. "I'm sorry because I shouldn't have snuck out of the house. I just knew that...you wouldn't want me to go."

Our conversation is going in loops and getting us nowhere in particular.

"What did he want?" I finally ask after taking a deep breath.

But before he can answer, I cut him off.

"Oh, wait, I know! He told you how much he and my mom miss me. He told you how mean I was to not answer Mom's calls, right? How inconsiderate. And if I just had, then they wouldn't have made up this ridiculous unforgivable thing?"

"Your mom and your dad are...seeing each other again."

"What?" I gasp.

"She cheated on him with some guy she used to date in high school."

"Apparently, they're working through their problems."

I walk around the room, my head thick with confusion.

"I don't understand why they did this," I whisper. "I really don't."

Jackson walks over to me and puts his arms around me.

I am still angry, but it feels good to have his body close to mine.

Suddenly, I crave him again.

The feeling comes out of nowhere and takes me by surprise.

I bite my lower lip to keep it at bay without much success.

Then I cave. I reach over to him and press my lips onto his.

Hard.

I kiss him like I want to hurt him, which I do. I'm angry with him, yet I yearn for him.

He kisses me back, his lips devouring mine.

But the more we kiss, the harder it is to pull away.

The craving for him is so strong, it's as if he's a drug.

When his hands leave my neck and trail down my body, I suddenly push him away.

"No, no, no." I jump away from him and walk toward the window.

I wrap my arms around my body and stare out at the meadow, my perfect snow angel, now crossed by rabbit's footsteps.

Jackson begins to talk.

I don't turn around to face him, just listen, looking away.

His voice is soft with an even keel, without an ounce of emotion.

He's not his advocate; he is just relaying what my father told him.

"He said that he misses you very much. He said that these years after Aspen's death have been the hardest in his life. But what made losing the ranch and Aspen even worse is that he lost his whole family after that as well. His wife left, and you moved away never to return."

I want to rebut, state my case.

Explain myself.

But I'd be talking to a ghost.

My father isn't here.

This is a one way conversation where I am only on the receiving end.

"A few months ago, he ran into your mom and they went out for a drink. And they've been inseparable ever since."

I shrug, shaking my head.

"He told me that they've been together their whole lives, Harley. And that they both made mistakes, but they also learned to forgive each other and move on. They didn't want to lose anymore time."

I clench my jaw.

It would be a lie to say that a part of me was relieved that they were back together.

As difficult as my mom is, the only person who ever tempered her tendencies is my dad.

He was always the one who was kind.

He was always the one who softened her up and made her a human being.

And in return, she supported him and his crazy ideas, though through clenched teeth.

"So...so, what about now?" I ask, finally turning around.

He looks me straight in the eye and gives me a shrug.

"He didn't say."

I furrow my brow. What does he mean he didn't say?

"He didn't go into it."

"So, what, you just talked to him about the past?"

"And the future."

I don't understand.

"He wanted to know what my intentions are with you."

I take a step back, completely surprised.

"Trust me, I was as shocked as you are. But he came right out and asked me. He said his little girl doesn't need anyone wasting her time."

"That doesn't sound like my dad," I say, shaking my head. "What did you say to him?"

Jackson takes a step closer to me. He lifts my chin up and looks directly into my eyes.

"I told him that I love you."

I blink.

"I love you, Harley."

CHAPTER 11 - JACKSON

WHEN I SEE HER...

The words just came out.

They weren't planned.

I hadn't given it much thought.

But when I was sitting there in that cozy coffee shop with the man who was responsible for bringing Harley into the world, and he asked me how I felt about her, I told him the truth.

Harold Burke is a talkative man with wispy, out of control hair, and patches on the elbows of his jacket.

When he comes in, he stomps his feet to get the snow off his boots, takes off his long puffy coat, and comes right over to me.

I extend my hand, but he embraces me with a big bear hug, even though he's not a very big man.

After ordering his coffee and a muffin the size of Wisconsin, he takes a seat across from me and apologizes.

"I'm so sorry that we had to meet under these terrible circumstances, and I want to thank you for taking the time to meet with me today."

"Thank you, Mr. Burke."

"Oh, please, call me Harold. Only my students call me Mr. Burke."

I nod. "What do you teach?"

"American History. Tenth grade. Government. Eleventh grade."

"That must be...a handful."

Given that I've never had the patience for kids, let alone teenagers, I have great admiration for those who make teaching their life.

"They are, but they're also incredibly fun. It's nice to be there to see them grow and learn and become the people that they are going to be."

"Where did you go to school?"

"University of North Carolina."

"Impressive. Are you from the south?"

"No, I'm actually from Pennsylvania. But I liked the campus when I took a tour so that's why I went there."

"What did you major in?"

"History. I actually wrote my senior thesis on how the Civil War became the Indian Wars and the devastation of the Native American nations in the Reconstruction Era and the colonization of the West."

"That's something that I'm quite familiar with," he says with a smile. "So, what is it that you do now? History majors tend to pursue careers in the law."

"Mine took me in a little different direction."

He is pleasantly surprised when I mention Minetta Media.

Apparently, he's an avid consumer of our content and is a big fan of a number of our podcasts.

We talk about that until it starts to feel like we are just buying time, dancing around the real reason I'm here.

But I don't push him.

Relationships between adult children and their parents are very complicated and the fact that he had reached out to me, a total stranger, is reason enough to let him bring it up in his own time.

"Did Harley tell you about the Burke Ranch?" he asks after we order another round of coffees.

I nod.

"It was our dream. Leslie's and mine. We didn't

come from much, spent most of our time in foster homes, actually that's where we met. When we were both seventeen. It wasn't a good place, so we decided to run away together and get married. We were so young."

I nod, amazed at how open he is being with a total stranger.

But maybe after awhile you just accept who you are and wear that face to the whole world without worrying about the consequences.

"We used to do this thing where we would drive around and look at rich people's houses. We'd look through real estate listings and find one house that we both loved and just go there. We'd find it on the map and drive around it, admiring it and sit on top of the car, imagining what our world would be like if it were ours.

"Quickly, we realized that what we both wanted was a ranch with acreage and lots of animals. Not to sell them or kill them or anything, just for them to be around us. Expensive pets, as it goes."

I smile.

"Then we started to make our way toward making our dreams a reality. We applied to the University of Montana, graduated. Leslie went to the police academy and I started studying for my teaching license."

I nod, hoping that he will tell me more about this rather than what is to come.

The beginning of stories, especially the ones you know are going to end badly are always so full of possibility.

"Well, you probably know the rest," he says suddenly, probably not wanting to go there either.

"I do."

"What you probably don't know though is that Leslie and I are back on, as the kids say. We got divorced but stayed in touch because after all of those happy years together, it was too hard not to. And then I ran into her at a bar and we got to talking and laughing and it was like no time had passed at all. It was like none of those bad things ever happened."

"I understand," I say.

"What I'm trying to say...in a very convoluted and not particularly direct way is that...I miss Harley. I miss my daughter."

His eyes are filling up with tears, and he rubs them with the back of his hand.

When he clears his throat, he turns to me and

asks, "Tell me, what are you doing to make her happy?"

"We didn't meet that long ago," I say, "but every moment that we have spent together has been... beyond any expectations."

I can see from the expression on his face that my propensity for understatement is lost on him.

If I don't want him to think I'm a total ass, then I'll have to be more direct.

"I was really lost when I met her. I had a lot of bad things happen in my life and I'd tucked myself away from the world to try to deal with it. Well, time passed and I didn't get better. I just got more...alone. And then Harley came along and changed everything."

"For the better?"

"For the best."

"She has that tendency. She can make anyone happy. But what about you? What are you doing in return?"

"I love her," I whisper.

The words spring out of me.

Even though it's the first time the thought has crossed my mind, it is the most natural thing in the world.

"I appreciate you saying that," Harold says, putting his hand on mine.

"I support her," I continue.

He squeezes my hand and gives me a smile.

"And I make her come to see her crazy family even though she will now be as mad at me as she is at you."

CHAPTER 12- JACKSON

WHEN I KISS HER...

*H*arley stares at me with her big wide hazel eyes.

The words 'I love you' just escaped my lips, knocking the wind out of her.

"You don't have to say anything in return. I just wanted to tell you how I feel."

Her small, delicate mouth parts in the middle.

She licks her lower lip and my body burns for hers.

I lift my chin to hers. Our lips collide.

I bury my hands in her hair.

It's soft and damp with an earthy scent that doesn't come from any shampoo bottle.

She is soft and snug in my arms and she pulls away only far enough to utter, "I love you, too."

I clutch her closer, wrapping my arms around hers.

Her breaths become mine and mine become hers.

Her hands are ice.

She slips them under my shirt and my back recoils for a moment before welcoming her in.

I'm restless and hungry for her.

All of her.

Right now.

That's what she does to me.

One touch and I have to have her.

Another touch and I morph into a beast who can't control his impulses.

With her chin tilted toward the ceiling, her long hair moves in waves.

I run my hands down the contours of her body.

I know every curve and every dip.

The more I feel, the greedier I become.

I have to have her.

But she's ahead of me.

She is already unbuttoning my shirt and taking off my pants.

Today, we do not wait to play a game.

Today, we do not take it slowly.

We burn for one another.

She lifts up her hands and I slip off her sweater.

She pulls off her leggings and jumps on top of me.

I catch her and we fall onto the couch.

My crotch becomes a knot of electricity. Her legs open wide and wrap around mine.

Our kisses become sloppy as we devour each other's mouths.

But before I come inside of her, I flip her over on her back.

I want her under me.

I cradle her head, burying my fingers in her hair.

My lips make their way down her body.

I pause slightly near the bottom of her neck, but then quickly make my way down toward the top of her breasts.

God, I love them.

Her nipples are small, the color of mocha.

They harden against my tongue.

I don't favor one breast over another, making my way across both to give each adequate attention.

As my mouth travels south, I watch as her belly button rises and falls with each quickened breath.

I run my hands down her thighs and press them deep inside of her.

77

Her body starts to move faster and faster and she gives out a quiet moan.

I press my lips in between her thighs and lick the most intimate part of her.

But before I can get any further, she closes her legs a little over my head and then pulls me up to her mouth.

"What's wrong?"

"I want you inside of me."

I reach for a condom and quickly slip it on as she tongues the back of my earlobe.

A moment later, her legs wrap tightly around my torso and she pushes me into her.

Our movements start out fast and get even faster.

We are feverish for one another.

We grasp onto each other's bodies as if we are falling and ride a wave that is all too short.

When it's all over, drenched in each other's sweat, we hold each other, unwilling to be the first to separate.

LATER THAT MORNING, after showering and getting dressed, we find ourselves back on the couch staring at the meadow of snow outside.

Big flakes are starting to fall, and the news broadcast predicts a blizzard.

I don't bring up Harold or Leslie but, by the way that Harley is staring into space, I know that they are not far from her mind.

"It was just so sunny," I point out. "I can't believe that the weather turned so quickly."

"There's an old saying in the Rockies. If you don't like the weather, wait twenty minutes."

I smile. "How long will this last?"

"Probably through the night. Maybe into tomorrow. The snow comes quick and fast here, but then the sun comes out again and it's as if nothing happened."

"Except for piles of it everywhere," I point out.

"Well, yeah, except for that."

I debate whether I should bring up the fact that if she wants to leave Montana today, we should probably hustle before it gets too dangerous to fly.

But I kind of want to buy some time.

I've never been in the West and there are things I want to see.

Besides, after talking to Harold, I feel bad just taking off on him without another word.

Without trying to talk to Harley again.

79

"We probably won't be able to fly home today," she says with a little smile.

"You don't seem too disappointed by that."

"Well, I kinda like this place," she says, looking around. "I never stayed in a chalet before."

"I'm glad that I can be of service."

"Are your services available tonight as well?"

I raise my eyebrows. "I'm at your beck and call, madam."

We sit in silence for a few minutes before she turns to me again.

"I think I have to meet with my dad."

CHAPTER 13 - HARLEY

SNOWED IN...

S now starts to fall in big thick flakes and I know that there's no way we are flying out of here today.

But that's okay.

As much as I wanted to leave immediately after the hospital fiasco, now something is holding me back.

I should at least see my dad.

While I stare out of the window, Jackson excuses himself to check his emails and do a little work.

He occupies the space at the end of the dining room table with his laptop and immediately shuts everything else out.

I, on the other hand, feel restless and unfocused.

My content writing job is ad-hoc, meaning that I

can write as many articles as I can in a day or not write any at all.

I just go to the website and choose one.

Once I get five-hundred words on the topic with a good introduction, conclusion, and three supporting paragraphs, my work is pretty much done.

Unfortunately, these last few days have really thrown me off track.

I open my computer and stare at the list of potential stories.

One is about electric plugs, another one is about getting into an ivy league school.

There's a huge list under a variety of topics, but none look that appealing.

That job requires rhythm and momentum, both of which are built over time.

Back home, with a strict writing schedule, I could pump out five to six articles a day pretty easily.

But here, my thoughts get away from me and no words come out when I start to type.

Glancing over, Jackson sees me struggling.

"What are you doing?"

"Trying to make some money." He knows a bit about my content writing job, the only steady position I had when we met.

"I thought you were working for me?"

Am I still?

Everything happened so quickly that I actually have no idea whether I still have that position.

"Well, you seemed busy, so I didn't want to bother you."

"Frankly, I don't really have much for you to do right now."

I nod. "I understand."

"It's not to say that you no longer have a job. Of course, you do."

"It's fine...I got by fine with this. I just need to focus and really work for a while today to get back on track." I rub my temples, trying to make the incessant headache that has suddenly creeped up disappear.

He walks over and puts his hand on my shoulder. "I'm not bullshitting you, Harley. I still want you to work for me."

"Well, you don't have any work for me to do and I have to pay rent at the beginning of the month."

"Please don't worry about that."

I look up at him incensed. "Are you serious?"

"I can give you the money. I'm rich, remember?"

He smiles that seductive, unassuming smile that makes my whole body tingle.

"That doesn't mean that I'm going to take your money. I have my own money and I can get by on it just fine," I say proudly.

Well, that's not exactly true.

But I have gotten by on it just fine.

Things are a bit more complicated now that Julie is no longer living with me and I have this enormous medical bill hanging over my head.

He glances at my screen and silently reads over the article topics.

"Harley, you're a writer, right?"

I nod.

"Is this what you want to spend your time doing?"

I shrug. "At least, I'm writing. I'm not very good at waitressing, I found that out the hard way."

"Yes, you are writing. But is this what you want to be writing?"

I roll my eyes.

"I'm not trying to be rude. I'm asking a legitimate question."

"No, of course not."

"Okay, then, now we're getting somewhere."

"Where?"

"Stay with me."

I take a deep breath and exhale it very slowly, wallowing in my exasperation.

"What would you write if you could write anything?"

"A novel," I say, without missing a beat.

"What kind?"

"I'm not sure yet, but something with a love story. Maybe about a normal girl who meets a dark, mysterious stranger who sweeps her off her feet?"

"That sounds like a really good story to me."

I shrug.

"What?"

"I've written a lot of stuff before. Short stories. Part of a young adult novel."

"And? Why didn't you finish?"

I stare at him without breaking eye contact.

"I submitted it to like a million literary agents. Okay, that's an exaggeration, but definitely fifty. I wrote fifty cover letters, each specifically tailored to them. I sent them the query letter, three chapters, and a synopsis. Everything that they require. I submitted my work to big names and non-existent names, people just starting out. And nothing. No one cared."

"So what?"

I look away in defeat.

"So...maybe it's not meant to be."

"Maybe they don't know what they're talking about? Did you ever consider that?"

I shake my head.

"You don't know that. You're just...taking my side."

"Okay, how about this, why don't you write a novel now? The one you mentioned you wanted to."

I blush and shake my head.

"I can't."

"Why not?"

"What would be the point? It will probably be rejected just like all of my other stuff."

He spins me around in my chair and gets down on one knee. Holding me by my shoulders, he leans in and asks, "Why even send it to them?"

"You want me to write a novel just for myself? And what, keep it in a drawer forever?"

"No." He smiles. "I want you to write this novel and publish it yourself. There are so many books on Amazon, Apple, Google Play, Barnes and Noble, and all of those other retailers that are independently published. And the readers? They don't care. The only thing they care about is that it's good and it's something they want to read. So, just say fuck it to the whole publishing industry and do it yourself."

CHAPTER 14 - HARLEY

WHEN HE PLANTS AN IDEA...

*D*IY?

Is that something that writers do?

I mean, of course, I've heard of self-publishing, but I had no idea that it was so...prominent and pervasive.

Jackson opens my computer and goes to Amazon.

Then he scrolls through the kindle store and points out all the books that are self-published.

"How do you know that these are self-published?"

"Well, the telltale sign is that they cost about half of a traditionally published ebook. You see, all of these books that are $6.99 and $5.99 and less? Those are all indie writers. And they all have people buying their books."

I sit back in my chair, astounded by what he has just revealed.

I spent so much of my time researching literary agents and publishing houses that I completely overlooked this entire field that has popped up to challenge their domination.

"So, how do you know so much about this?"

"I'm in the content creation business, remember? Minetta Media acquired two podcasts about self-publishing. They're run by two very successful indie authors and they really know what they're talking about."

I stare at the screen with a newfound zest for creativity.

I was so depressed to not hear back from any of the agents I'd contacted that I really put the whole thing out of my mind.

And now? Now...life is full of possibilities again.

"This sounds amazing," I admit.

"But?" Jackson asks, sensing my trepidation.

"But...I still have to write to make money. I mean, I can't rely on people just buying my book when I publish it."

"No, of course not. It will take awhile for you to

find readers, actually. And you will have to learn how to do some marketing and run advertising to promote the book. It's a long journey after you finish the book."

"So, you see...it's just not something I can invest my time in now given that I have to make money. However, meager and ridiculous."

Jackson smiles at me again. His eyes light up and I know that he has another idea.

"What? What are you thinking?" I pull him toward me and put my mouth on his. He licks me back, but pulls away.

"What if instead of spending time writing that useless crap that provides very little value to anyone except to the company for click bait...what if instead of doing that, I paid you to do this instead? To work on your novel."

I shake my head no.

"That's...not fair."

"To whom?"

"To...everyone out there. I mean, you supporting my writing like that?"

"I want to, Harley. I think you have something special inside of you. And I want the world to see that. I want the world to read your books."

I think about that for a moment. The fact that he

even offered to do something like that is beyond generous. And it's everything that I ever wanted ever since I was a little girl. But can I really accept it?

"Okay, I mean...maybe," I finally say.

"Maybe?"

"Under one condition." He waits for me to state it.

"I can write whatever I want. You don't have a say in it at all."

"Of course." He nods his head. "I want to point out that you did not have that arrangement with your content writing job, but you are putting this restriction on me. But, fine."

He smiles and starts laughing in the middle of the sentence. He pulls me close to him and kisses me again. His hands trail up and down my body and I feel myself starting to burn for him.

I need to stay strong. "And if I want to write about sex or whatever else I can think of, I'm going to do that."

"You're going to write about sex? Oh my God, I had no idea. I would've offered you this deal when we first met."

I laugh. Last night, I told him about my history as a sex blogger, a virgin sex blogger, and he thought that was the funniest thing he'd ever heard.

"Well, now that you have a little bit more experience, I can't wait to see what you come up with."

I laugh, climb on top of him, and hit him in the head with a pillow. He quickly flips me over and presses his lips to mine.

UNFORTUNATELY, our little pillow fight ends with a PG-13 rating.

No sex.

Just a lot of good making out and heavy petting, as they used to say. Jackson has a conference call to get to and there's no time for anything more.

As he talks to Avery on the computer, I put on my earphones, put on my favorite instrumental playlist of popular songs, and open a new document on my computer.

I peruse through my journal and read the sketches that I wrote about the reclusive billionaire who lives alone in his mansion.

They were based on Jackson, but they're also not him at all.

That's what fiction is.

It starts out based on some kernel of truth, but

then the author lets her imagination run wild and the character suddenly becomes someone else completely new.

Where should this story go, I wonder?

If it's a love story then it's simple.

They meet, they fall in love, they have problems, they overcome their problems, and they end up together.

Or not.

Though I'm partial to the ones that end well.

I turn back to my computer and start to type.

I start with a list of scenes.

The beginning.

Who is he?

Who is she?

How do they meet?

What is their first night together like?

And as I type, the words start to flow out of me.

One after another. I lose track of time.

After a brief outline is complete, I take the first scene and jump right in.

There's no better time than right now, right?

Somewhere on my tenth or is it twelfth page, twilight starts to fall.

My eyes briefly wander over to Jackson, who to

my surprise is no longer at his computer but is reading something on his phone on the couch.

I don't watch him for long because I have my characters to get back to.

They are aching for me to continue their story.

It is pitch black outside when I finally decide to take a break.

My hands are throbbing from hitting the keys too fast and too hard and my neck hurts, but I don't care.

"Wow, I really lost you there for a bit," Jackson says. I smile. "Thank you...thank you for inspiring me."

CHAPTER 15 - HARLEY

WHEN I MEET WITH HIM...

*I*t snows all day and all night, and the sun doesn't show up until the following afternoon.

The roads are still just being cleared, but my father insists on coming anyway.

I'm now communicating with him through Jackson who arranges a meeting.

It was originally going to be in town at the same coffee shop where they'd met, but then he thought that everyone would be more comfortable at our house.

He ordered a lot of food from a couple of different restaurants and is just putting it into bowls and arranging it all on the island when my father rings the doorbell.

"Aren't you going to answer it?" Jackson asks. That snaps me out of my trance and I go to get the door.

It's hard to say how I feel about seeing my father again.

At first, I was excited.

I did miss him after all of this time apart.

Nothing happened between us so there was no reason for me to feel any negativity toward him.

At least until I got here and discovered she was a part of the worst con in history.

I mean, what the hell were they thinking?

Agh, I feel my blood starting to boil again and that's not why I agreed to meet with him today.

I open the door and am greeted by a man who looks a lot happier than I remember him being in a long time.

He gives me and Jackson warm hugs and puts the two large bags of groceries on the table next to all the takeout.

"I wasn't sure what you were doing for dinner, so I wanted to bring a couple of salads and chips and snacks."

I mumble a barely audible thank you as I take a moment to take him in.

He looks a lot like that man that I remember existed when Aspen was still alive.

He has a wide smile on his face, bright white teeth, a tan from hiking and skiing and spending a lot of time outdoors.

There aren't many wrinkles on his face, but the few that have popped up are ingrained into thick laugh lines.

"Let me have a look at you." He gives me another hug and then holds me out with outstretched arms as he looks me up and down the way parents do to toddlers.

I laugh and push him away, but he pulls me in close.

"So, I met your fella," Dad says. "He's one charming man. Much like myself."

I laugh.

My dad has always had a way of lightening the mood, no matter what was going on.

I'm glad that he hasn't lost that, or rather that he has recently recovered that ability.

Jackson says that it will be a few minutes before dinner is ready and pours us each some drinks.

I take my wine and he takes his whiskey to the large recliners near the fireplace.

We sit across from one another and look at each other for a few minutes without saying a word.

"How are you?" Dad is the first to break the silence.

"I'm fine."

"You look great."

I nod. "Seems like Jackson really loves you."

I blush a little.

I was never one of those girls who felt comfortable talking to her parents about her relationships.

"Well, it's very new, but yes, I love him, too."

"He better not break your heart," Dad says loud enough for Jackson to hear.

"I'm afraid she'll break mine before that happens," Jackson pipes in.

On one hand, I like how close and chummy Jackson has gotten with my dad after only one meeting, but that also makes me somewhat jealous.

I haven't had that kind of lighthearted and fun relationship with him for a very long time.

And I wish it was something that I could have, too.

But at the same time, I can't just gloss over everything that has happened or everything that we've been through.

He asks me about my work and my writing and I fill him in on some of the details.

The novel is too soon to mention, so I focus on my freelance writing jobs instead.

He listens carefully, asking questions and never once bringing up the fact that I work online and that I could do that work from much cheaper places in the world than Manhattan.

I know that he's biting his tongue, and I appreciate that.

Conversation drifts to his work and his students.

Surprisingly, he has as much passion for teaching now as he did when he was just getting started.

He isn't jaded or annoyed with the bored students; he takes that as a challenge.

If no one wants to read the books that he assigns like Shakespeare or Hawthorne, he makes it his personal mission to make the books relevant to the kids' lives.

"How long do you think you will continue teaching?"

I skate around the question of retirement because we both know that he could've retired already, except that he'd lost everything in the fire.

Everything but a job and a paycheck.

"I'm not sure. But I don't have any plans for stopping quite yet. Not while there are still kids who don't know who Mercutio is."

I laugh. "Dad, there will always be kids who don't know who Mercutio is."

"I guess my job will never be done then. And I count myself lucky for that. Not everyone can say that their job will always be of use."

I nod.

Yep, the man's right.

One short moment of silence is quickly filled up with conversations on a number of other topics.

Current events.

Politics.

Pop culture.

My dad is pretty well versed in all of those things and actually knows a lot more about what's going on in music and Hollywood than I do since he likes to take an interest in his kids' interests.

We talk about practically everything under the moon except for *that*.

Why did he lie to bring me here to Montana, and if it wasn't her idea, then why did he go along with her lie?

The food is ready and we grab a bit of everything from the plates, which are set up buffet style.

When we sit down at the table, I can't skirt around the edges of the issue anymore.

I've suddenly had my fill of small talk. It's enough.

"Um, Dad?" I ask, taking a bite of my salad. "Now that we've caught up on practically everything...don't you think we should talk about what happened?"

The question catches him off guard.

He has never been one for confrontation, and the way he makes nice is by just acting friendly and hoping that it will just go away.

Well, it's not going to go away that easily.

Not this time.

I don't want to let it go until I get some answers.

Dad looks at Jackson almost pleading, asking him for support.

"Do you want some privacy?" Jackson asks instead.

"No, definitely not," Dad says. "The thing is, honey, is that I don't really have a good explanation."

"So...how did it come up? I mean, who thought of this in the first place?"

"Your mother did. It was her idea, and initially I didn't want to go along with it, but she sort of wore me down. She kept telling me that it was the only way we could get you to come back here. You weren't answering her calls at all. You were barely talking to me."

A little pang of anger builds in the pit of my stomach, but he raises his hand to stop me from saying anything.

"I'm not blaming you. I'm just explaining where she, we, were coming from."

I feel my face turn to ice. "Why didn't you just show up in New York?"

"I wanted to...but Mom was...afraid."

"Afraid?"

"Afraid that you would close the door in her face. She will never admit it in a million years, Harley, you know that, but she was afraid. She doesn't deal with rejection well. So, when you stopped answering her calls...she just...shut down."

I ask him more questions and get pretty much the same answers back.

I wonder if that has to do with the fact that it's the truth or if he's just repeating the same lies over and over.

Either way, we're not really getting anywhere.

"Tell me," my dad suddenly says, "tell me how I can make this better."

I shake my head.

The truth is that I have no idea.

It's so...fucked up.

I understand where he's coming from. I sort of get why they did what they did, but it doesn't change how hurt I am.

I don't really know if I can get over something like this.

But at the same time, what choice do I have?

They are the only parents I have, the only ones I will ever have.

And spending this time with my dad really did remind me of the good times that we once had. It wasn't that long ago that we laughed until we cried.

It wasn't that long ago that everything felt...normal.

The way it should.

Hell, even better.

The way it is in the movies.

Dad stays through dinner and then leaves.

He takes off on a good note; we don't talk about Mom or anything that brought me here: instead, we talk exclusively about skiing.

I haven't been since I moved to New York and it is one of those real Montana things that I miss with all of my heart.

There is nothing like skiing the Rockies - the snow is like powder, the skies are bright blue, and the sun is almost always shining brightly even if it's ten degrees below outside.

When Dad leaves, nothing is really resolved, but something is mended a bit.

The feeling that I have toward him now has less to do with anger and more just disappointment.

If I can ever put it out of my mind completely, then everything will be fine again. That is if I'm capable of doing that.

THE FOLLOWING MORNING, the snow starts to melt.

The roads have all been cleared, the major ones anyway, and Jackson asks me to show him around my favorite haunts.

I suggest a few local points of interest, but he

mainly wants to drive around and look at the mountains.

I take him to the Bitterroot River and he falls in love.

I nearly freeze my butt off standing here watching the snow banks and the trees surrounding its banks.

"You know, it's much nicer in the summer," I point out.

"We'll have to come then."

I shake my head and smile.

That's not exactly what I meant.

As he stands in awe admiring the towering pines and the eagles circling high above, he says, "Tell me about it in June then."

"What do you mean?"

"You said it's much nicer in the summer. Describe it."

I close my eyes and try to remember how the grass smells as it grows, free of worries of ever being mowed.

"Summer sets in quickly here, just like any other season. One day it's cold and wet and the next it's hot and dry and it stays like that for three months. The sidehills get so green, it hurts your eyes to look at them. Everything seems to speed up. The insects buzz louder and faster. The people ride around in every direction trying to use up every last minute of the day."

When I open my eyes, I am immediately greeted by the whiteness and the austerity of winter, which has its own beauty.

"That sounds...beautiful. Will you come back with me this summer?"

"And if I say no?"

"I guess I'll just come by myself. I'm sure your dad will be happy to show me around."

I laugh. That I am certain of.

"Okay, let's go," Jackson says, placing his hand on my shoulder. "You look like you're about to turn into an icicle."

"Thank God! I thought you'd never ask." We race back to the car and ask the driver to turn the heat up.

Jackson wraps his arms around me, in an effort to warm me up even faster. After a few minutes, I finally start to thaw.

"Where to?" the driver asks.

"What else do you want to see?" I ask Jackson, blowing warm air on my frozen hands.

"The Burke Ranch."

CHAPTER 17 - HARLEY

WHEN I GO BACK...

*a*s soon as those words come out of his mouth, my world comes to a standstill.

No.

There's no way that I am going back there.

I haven't been there since Aspen's funeral.

It's a place that I intend to keep in my memories forever.

It has hurt me way too much over the years and being there in real life will just make it completely unbearable to breathe.

I tell Jackson all of this and he nods understandingly.

"What if you go there and discover that it doesn't actually hold any power over you? What if it's just a place?"

"But it's not."

He shrugs.

The driver again asks where to and I tell him to take us home.

Reluctantly, Jackson agrees, and we make our way over the winding roads back to the chalet without saying a word.

"Isn't it enough that I met with my dad?" I ask. "That was huge for me. If it weren't for you, I doubt that I would have."

"I'm glad you did. If it weren't for you, I wouldn't be sitting here at all." He looks out of the window and suddenly I realize just how much progress he has actually made.

In all of this commotion, I had completely forgotten to ask him how he's feeling about...not being in his house all day and all night.

So, I do.

"I actually feel fine," Jackson says. "Much better than I ever thought I would. I thought that I would feel claustrophobic and out of control, but it's actually very relaxing here. There aren't too many people. No one is shouting. No one is rushing around. There's very little traffic. And back at our house? It's...heaven."

I'm glad that I was able to be there for him.

I still have a hard time imagining what it would be like to never go outside for almost four years, but as soon as we pull up to our mountain cabin, as Jackson calls it, the prospect of going inside and not seeing anyone else for a year or two sounds...marvelous.

"Wait, before we go in..." Jackson places his hand on mine. "The reason I want you to take me to the Burke Ranch is that I want to see it with my own eyes. I want to see this place that has such an important hold on your family. On you and your history."

I clench my jaw and think about it for a moment.

Jackson sits back and waits.

"Fine," I finally cave.

I'm not so much giving into his request as going along with the same feeling that I have deep inside of me.

That place has been a dark cloud over me for all of my adult life.

And it's time that it isn't anymore.

THE ROAD LEADING to the ranch is desolate.

It's in a valley, following a small two-lane highway down a snow-covered plain.

The few houses that existed in this area prior to the fire have all been abandoned and now the ranch, or what remains of it, stands alone against the starkness of the elements.

The highway starts to meander a little around the hills and I know that we're getting close.

I tell the driver to turn at the next left, even though it's unmarked.

It's unofficially named Burke Road, which splinters off suddenly and heads straight into the mountains in the distance.

We drive for a few miles, but the mountains seem just as far as they were when we started.

When we get to the end, we pull up to a large wooden gate, which I remember my parents fought over.

It was very important for my mom to have a traditional Western gate.

Two looming poles on either side of the road supporting a large beam laying across them.

I can't remember exactly how much this gate cost, but it was a significant portion of the budget, enough to make my otherwise nonchalant Dad cringe.

Ironically, this is the only thing that survived the fire.

We park near the gate and go on foot the rest of the way.

The road the rest of the way isn't plowed.

"So, this is it," I say when we finally make it up the hill and move toward the place where the house once stood.

All that's left is the foundation and even that is hidden under feet of snow.

"Where?" he asks, looking around.

"The porch was about here. The garage over there."

Jackson looks around at the mountains hugging almost every curve for as far as the eye can see.

The sun is starting to set, painting the sky with splashes of pink and reds.

"This is a very beautiful spot," he says after a moment. "I've never seen anything quite like it."

I shrug and hang my head. I'm not really sure what to say to that.

"Do your parents still own the land?"

"Yeah, I think so."

"That's something."

I shrug, not particularly convinced.

They do have to pay taxes on it every year, and it's not exactly something they can easily afford.

And for what?

Just some land where they were once happy?

I mean, what's the point of hanging onto it?

"Do you think they will ever try to rebuild it? I mean, now that they're together?"

"Even if they do, they don't have the money. But honestly I have no idea what they're thinking."

"What about you?" Jackson asks, lifting my chin up to the sky. "Do you miss this place?"

I look around.

It's weird being here again.

But the truth is that as beautiful as it was, I have very few memories here which are any good.

Some yes, but most of my best memories are from that other house we lived in that they sold to buy this one.

This was their dream, not mine. To me, this place is just too full of ghosts to yearn for it again.

"Where's Aspen?" Jackson asks and a little piece of my heart splinters off.

CHAPTER 18 - HARLEY

WHEN DARKNESS DESCENDS...

The main reason why this place gives me dread is that my parents decided to bury Aspen here.

They were overcome with grief and there was no talking them out of it.

This was their home, their life. It was their everything.

And once they got permission from the state to make a cemetery plot here, they did.

They also talked about making arrangements to be buried here with him, something that I thought would happen soon after Aspen's death.

I never talked about this with anyone, but for awhile there I thought that I was going to be an orphan.

My parents were so buried in their own sadness that I didn't see a way for them to come out.

It was around that time that they started to plan their own funerals by arranging for adjoining plots next to his.

But time passed and somehow, everyone kept breathing.

That's the thing about life, though.

If you aren't careful, you can spend your whole time here on earth just breathing and not doing much living.

I existed that way for a while, too, until I came to New York.

But my parents?

I don't know.

My dad seems happier than he has been in years, and I hope that isn't just some act that he's pulling.

I hope that it's true. I hope that he actually is happy. I hope they both are.

"His grave is right there near the tree line, overlooking the bluff."

It takes us a good ten minutes to get there.

Each step has to make it through three feet of virginal snow, untouched by anyone, and extremely difficult to get through.

When we finally get there, my eyes are filled with tears.

He has a large black headstone marking his grave with his name and dates of birth and death.

On the top is a little etching of his face taken from a photograph with his favorite stuffed animal.

I haven't stood here since the funeral and being here again I suddenly realize how lonesome it is here.

It's all good and well that my parents arranged for adjoining gravesites, but what does that matter now?

He's here all alone.

There isn't another soul for miles and he wasn't the type of kid who liked solitude.

"They shouldn't have done this," I mumble through my tears.

"Done what?"

"They shouldn't have buried him here. He's here all alone. It would be one thing if they were rebuilding that house and were still living here, but they're not. He's all alone in this...tundra."

My whole face is wet from my sobs and I lean on Jackson until he's practically holding me up.

"If they had just...cremated him. Then I could've

had a part of him with me always. I would've taken him to New York with me and anywhere else I went. And now, if I want to be with him, I have to come here...to this God-forsaken place."

Jackson wraps his arms tightly around me and holds me until I am ready to go.

My tears continue to flow but I can't be here anymore.

When I finally turn to leave, something within me pushes me back toward the grave.

"I can't...just leave him here all alone, Jackson."

"Yes, you can because he's not here."

I look up at him, surprised. "His body may be here, but his spirit isn't. I'm not a very religious person, but I know that to be true."

I nod.

"I mean, would you hang around here if you could be traveling through multiple dimensions at once?"

"He's probably on the beach somewhere warm playing in the sand. He always loved the water," I say, smiling out of the corner of my mouth.

Jackson lifts up my chin and kisses me with his cold lips.

I kiss him back, but only slightly.

"No, that's not good enough. I'm never going to let you get away with a paltry kiss like that," he says, pressing his mouth onto mine and showing me how it's done. I laugh and agree to the challenge.

CHAPTER 19 - JACKSON

WHEN WE GO BACK...

While Harley is still asleep, I take my coffee outside.

Standing on the wraparound porch that looks out onto the valley out back, I watch as an eagle flies in circles above my head.

Somewhere in the distance, I hear the yelp of a coyote followed by the long howl of a lone wolf.

It's early still, and the sun hasn't quite risen above the tree line.

There are only inklings of it in the form of mango and blush colors that paint the sky at the edges.

I take a deep breath, exhaling slowly.

A little rabbit with a cottontail sits under the

pine next to the porch and holds one of the carrots that I left for him there.

At first, he looks up at me with suspicion, but then relaxes a bit and enjoys his food.

As I watch morning unfold here, what's different between this place and New York?

Back home, I have to hole myself up in my mansion to block out the outside world.

I was searching for solitude and quietness that I could never really find.

Except when I got here.

Now, all I want to do is stay outside and revel in the beauty that's all around me.

Harley wants to go back as soon as possible, but I wouldn't mind staying here for another few days or a month or even a lifetime.

I don't blame her though.

Her experience of this land is completely different than mine.

There's too much baggage here and there's too much hurt.

As much as I tried to help her make peace between her and her father, I know that it will take awhile for them to rebuild their relationship, if that ever happens. It's up to Harley and she is still full of anger and hate over what her parents did.

My chest tightens at the memory of her seeing her mother again at that hospital.

Within a matter of seconds, she went from being excited and happy that she was alright to being in shock.

And now, all she wants is an answer.

But the answer that Harold is giving her isn't enough.

I know that he's not lying.

They made up that story to get her to come and meet them on their terms.

They were afraid of going to New York and being rejected face-to-face.

Yet, they needed to see her.

It's not a satisfying answer, but it's the only one she will get.

I'm not sure it's enough for her.

Time will tell, I guess.

Harley calls her father on the way to the airport to tell him that we are leaving.

Last night, she made the decision that she does not want to see her mother or to even speak to her.

I hear the disappointment in Harold's voice that she is leaving without even saying goodbye to him in person.

But she promises to see him again and even invites him to New York.

That seems to satisfy him for now.

The flight back is uneventful, and Harley buries her head in her computer, hard at work on her new project.

I'm glad that my encouragement has led her to pursue her writing again.

I know that it's the one thing that she really wants to do and I know that she can be really good at it.

I've read bits of her old blog; she really has a way with words and language. All she needed was a push in the right direction.

The thought that she would give up her passion, just because some literary agent decided that her writing wasn't good enough for them, makes my blood run hot.

Even now, sitting here on the couch of my private plane and watching her work feverishly at the table next to mine, I can't help but clench my fists in anger.

Who the hell do they think they are?

They rejected her because they didn't think that they could sell her books. "She wasn't a good fit for them at this time," as they like to say.

Well, she'll show them.

If only these traditional publishing hacks knew how many successful indie authors there are out there now.

If only other writers knew how much more money they could make publishing their work themselves rather than going through a publisher.

Online retailers like Amazon pay a royalty of 70%, meaning that they only keep thirty for publishing and the writer gets seventy.

In traditional publishing, the writer gets ten percent and that's after the publisher recoups any money they spent on marketing.

Of course, there are additional responsibilities that come with publishing your own work yourself.

You become the publisher and that means you pay for editing, cover design, and marketing.

You have to build your own brand and it takes time to get readers to find out about you.

But in the end, you have all the freedom.

You are in charge of your career.

You publish a book whenever you think it's done and ready instead of waiting for approvals.

You publish the book you want and chance that there will be readers who will connect with it.

As a result of eBooks, e-readers, and Amazon,

publishing is in its Golden Age right now, and with a lot of hard work and determination, I know that Harley can find herself a place within it.

I finish my cup of coffee and ask the flight attendant to bring me another.

For the first time, in a long time, I'm having a hard time focusing on my own work.

It was always something that was front and center in my life and now, suddenly, it's not.

It's not that it's not important anymore, of course, it is.

It's just that I now have to split my attention when all I want to do is focus it entirely on her.

My phone buzzes and I look at the screen. It's a text message from Phillips.

Call me. We have a major problem.

CHAPTER 20 - JACKSON

SOMETHING'S WRONG...

I call Phillips back immediately.

She answers in a frazzled voice, which I have never heard before.

Nothing phases her.

Whenever we would have a slow quarter, she was always the one who would make plans to make up for it the following quarter.

Whenever any crisis arose, she was always the one to fix it in a calm manner.

"How soon can you get back to New York?"

"I'll be there by three. What's wrong?"

"They've arrested Swanson."

It takes me a moment to remember who Swanson is.

"For what?"

"Securities fraud."

My heart drops and all the blood drains from my face. Harley stops typing and looks up at me.

"What's wrong?" she whispers. I shake my head, not now.

"Apparently, he has been running a Ponzi scheme."

I don't believe it. Phillips goes over more details, and my head starts to spin as I try to remember exactly how much money I have invested with the Swanson Securities Group.

"Okay, call me if you learn anything more." I hang up the phone and watch as it drops to the floor.

Harley picks it up and comes to sit down next to me.

She wants to know what happened, but my mouth is completely dry.

A desert.

When I open my lips to speak, no words come out. I reach for the bottle of water on the table and she intercepts it and hands it to me. For a moment, I'm satiated but the next it's not enough.

I finish the bottle and turn toward her. Finally, I am able to speak and tell her the whole story.

As a young man, Richard Swanson worked as a

lifeguard, saving every penny so he could invest it all into the stock market.

He built his firm from five thousand dollars to the most elite boutique investment group in New York.

He was known for a very specific investment strategy, which many money managers considered too safe to make any real money.

He was known for purchasing blue-chip stocks and then taking option contracts on them. But the details of the strategy changed, of course.

When I first considered investing my money with him, my research showed that in the 1970s, he placed invested funds into convertible arbitrage positions in large-cap stocks, promising investment returns of eighteen to twenty percent.

But by the eighties, he began using futures contracts on the stock index, and then placing options on futures during the stock market crash of 1987. So, when everyone else lost money, he actually got rich.

Given how elite his group was, Swanson did not actively recruit new members or promise anyone high returns in return for their investment.

Instead, he kept his clientele exclusive and on a

must-know basis, and offered a lot more modest and steady returns than many other firms.

That was one of the reasons I decided to go with him.

Once Minetta made some serious money, I started looking for investment opportunities and Wall Street is, of course, the first thing that came to mind.

"Lots of investment groups were looking to get their hands on my money, and most offered a lot more money than Swanson. I knew a lot of wealthy people who invested a lot of money with him over the years and they saw good, steady returns."

"Were the returns always good?" Harley asks.

"There was a natural variation to them over the months, but in general they were pretty steady at around twelve percent. It was all...as expected."

She nods, putting her hand around my shoulder.

I pick up my phone again and search the news.

But I don't even have to type his name into the search bar, it's the headline story everywhere.

PROSECUTORS ESTIMATE *the size of the fraud to be $64.8 billion*

.   .   .

SWANSON SECURITIES GROUP has liabilities of approximately $50 billion

"WHAT DOES THIS MEAN EXACTLY?" Harley asks.

"It means that according to him, he owes people fifty and according to the prosecutors, he owes them close to sixty-five. Billion."

"Five thousand clients," Harley reads. "That's a lot of people."

"It's much more than that. I'm one client, but the Maine Teachers' Pension fund is another." I scan one article after another. "Apparently, he targeted pension funds a lot since they are institutional investors with a lot of money sitting around."

"That's terrible."

I nod.

"So...what exactly is a Ponzi scheme?" she asks after a moment.

"It means he wasn't investing any money at all. He was just taking on new investors to pay the old ones."

I scan another article and summarize the findings.

"Apparently, recently he focused a lot on private foundations because of the five percent payout rule, which requires them to pay out five percent of their funds each year. They never took out more than that and that protected him from sudden withdrawals, perpetuating his fraud."

"That's how he was able to pay his debts to prior investors, with new money," Harley says. I give her a slight nod.

She doesn't ask anymore questions for a while; we sit in silence as my world crashes around me.

I try to do anything but calculate exactly how much money I have invested with them, but I can't keep myself from counting.

That was the money that I was using to keep Minetta Media afloat. It made money initially, but with the big expansion, it acquired a lot of debt as well.

Debt that I thought I could pay with the money from this fund. But now, it's all gone.

And then there's Woodward.

It will take him a few phone calls to find out that I had my assets tied up with Swanson and once he knows that, he will never give me the deal that he was going to give me before.

Why would he?

Suddenly, I'm wounded.

Desperate.

Bleeding.

About to die.

He could wait for the whole thing to collapse and buy it later for parts, or he could invest in it now under terrible terms, for me anyway.

Harley turns to me and takes my hand in hers. "It's going to be okay," she whispers, even though we both know that's a lie.

"Ask me," I say after a moment.

"What?"

"Ask me the question that you are dying to know the answer to."

She looks away and then directly at me.

"How much did you have invested with Swanson?"

"Six hundred million dollars."

CHAPTER 21 - JACKSON

DARKNESS DESCENDS...

J've known the answer to her question ever since Phillips first called me.

But saying the words out loud made it real.

Six hundred million dollars.

There's a small chance, of course, that there will be restitution paid and some of the money will be reimbursed.

But that will not happen until after a lengthy trial.

His assets will be sold, but there's no way that he has enough to cover everyone's losses.

Fiction.

Everything he did was made up.

He hasn't made any real investments since the

late nineties; all he did was pay new investors with old money.

After dropping Harley off at Julie's place, I ask Mr. Garbo to drive me home.

I want to be alone now.

I need to be alone again.

Harley wants to come stay with me, to comfort me, to be here for me, but I push her away.

Not now.

I can't be around people now, not even her.

I can see that her feelings are hurt when I give her a small peck on the cheek, but it's all the affection that I can force myself to show at this moment.

When I walk back into my home, I pour myself a glass of whiskey and place the glass canister under my arm.

I head straight upstairs into my office.

This is not a place I go to often, because of what happened here, but tonight it's the only place that I can be.

The walls are lined with built in, dark wooden bookcases.

I sit down on the leather couch, which was her favorite place to sit and play while I worked and I pick up the blanket that she used to wrap around herself when the room got cold.

There's a fireplace in the corner and I flick it on, bathing the room in a warm glow.

It's strange where your thoughts go when you lose so much money.

Suddenly, my heart breaks, but not for my wealth, for someone else I lost, right here in this room.

It has been rebuilt to look exactly like it did before, but this place is not the original room that she played in.

Before I had this whole life, I had Lila.

She was the sweetest little girl in the world and she was my everything.

Her mother took off soon after her birth and is now married to some royal in Europe.

As hard and fraught as that relationship was, it did result in creating someone I gave my whole heart to.

My Lila.

I take a picture frame off the shelf with her image in it.

This was taken only a few months before she died.

She's sitting on a big rock in Central Park and laughing as always.

I wipe away the tears that run down my cheeks and put her picture away.

Even after all of these years, I still can't really bear to think about her for too long.

That's one of the reasons I haven't told Harley about her yet, even though she was brave enough to tell me about Aspen.

The darkness that we have faced in our pasts seems to mirror one another's.

She, of all people, would understand the pain I feel now, but she is the one person I can't tell.

Yet.

It's almost five and Phillips is blowing up my phone, but I can't bring myself to talk to her yet.

I just keep looking around this room and missing my little girl.

If she were alive now, all that money wouldn't matter so much.

It would just be something unfortunate that happened.

It's a lot to lose, of course, especially in a fraud, but I've never been one who cared much for material possessions.

But with Lila gone, this house has become

something of a museum for my love for her. She loved this house. She loved its grandness and its beauty. She loved rollerskating down its large hallways and she loved that she could play hide and seek here, and the fact that no one could ever find her.

The reality of what losing all of this money means is settling in somewhere in the back of my mind.

When I bought this house, I took out a mortgage, which I quickly paid off.

But then when Minetta Media started running into cash flow problems and my money was tied up with Swanson's Group, I took out another mortgage on this place.

That gave me enough cash to keep the company afloat and even profitable.

But we kept needing the money during our process of expansion and I kept reinvesting whatever profits we had back into the company, rather than paying off my mortgage.

Since I was the sole owner, I never took a large salary in order to reinvest further in the business.

And now, with all of that money gone?

My salary isn't nearly enough to cover the mortgage payments.

I look around the room that Lila loved so much and finally come to terms with this reality.

I am going to have to sell this house.

But given how large it is, finding a buyer will be quite difficult and time-consuming.

What choice do I have?

It's either sell this house or Minetta.

"Phillips, sorry it took me a bit to call you back. Is there any other news?"

"No," she says gravely.

"Okay, that's fine. We have to start making some decisions."

"How about we talk about taking the company public again?"

CHAPTER 22 - HARLEY

WHEN I GET HOME...

The flight back from Missoula is a blur.

At first, I'm busy working on my tenth chapter of the novel and then Jackson's whole world collapses.

Losing that much money is...devastating.

When he hears the news, his normally olive skin turns completely white and his jaw clenches and doesn't relax until he drops me off at Julie's.

I want to come up and stay with him, but he pushes me away. He says he wants to be alone and that frightens me.

I don't want him to do anything stupid.

People who lose a lot of money can sometimes become consumed by that loss.

To the point of hurting themselves.

As I ride in the elevator, I debate with myself whether I should come right out and ask him to call me immediately if he has even an inkling of wanting to end his life.

But another part of me doesn't want to plant the idea in his head. If that hasn't occurred to him in the first place, the last thing I want to do is to bring it up.

I talked to Julie last night to update her on everything that happened in Montana and she welcomes me with open arms and a hundred apologies.

"You really have nothing to apologize for," I say, dropping off my bag in my room.

"But I was the one who told you that your father called."

"And I would've done the exact same thing in your place. I mean, what were you supposed to do? Not tell me that my mom was in a car accident and critically injured?"

She shrugs. "How could've anyone known that she made it all up. I mean...who the fuck does that to anyone, let alone their own kid?"

Julie shakes her head in disgust.

She asks me about the rest of the trip and I fill her in on the details.

"Well, at least you had a good time with your dad

and showing the ranch to Jackson must've been...something."

"Yeah, it was...something."

Even though all of that only happened yesterday, it suddenly feels as if it was years ago.

"What's wrong?"

I shake my head.

"What happened? Did you and Jackson get into a fight?"

"No, nothing like that."

"What?"

I don't know how much of this I should tell her, but it's all over the news.

Some of Swanson's biggest investors were already named in the press and if Jackson wasn't named yet, he probably will be soon.

"Have you heard about the Swanson thing?"

She nods. "Logan's father was invested in that fund. He lost a lot of money."

"Well, Jackson did, too."

Julie's mouth drops open as I fill her in on some of the details.

"So, how much did he lose?"

"A lot. I'm not sure exactly, but it's a significant amount."

As much as I want to, I can't tell her the number. It's not my place and it's none of her business.

A few minutes later, Logan calls and Julie excuses herself and disappears into their bedroom.

I make myself comfortable on the couch and pick up a magazine to flip through.

Anything to take my mind off the mess of thoughts that are swirling around in my head.

***

I must've fallen asleep because I suddenly wake up to loud yelling.

"You can just go fuck yourself then!"

"No, I don't want to hear it."

"I can't believe you did this to me. You are such a liar!"

It takes me a moment to realize what's going on. It's Julie and she's yelling at someone on the phone.

"What an asshole!" she says, slamming the door shut. It makes a loud thump sound, echoing all around the apartment.

"What happened?"

"We were on Skype and I could see the rumpled bed behind him at his hotel room. And then someone moved. It was a girl. She fucking got up, completely nude, and walked out of the frame."

"Oh my God," I say, covering my mouth with my hand.

"Can you believe that? She was right there and he just...forgot. Forgot that he was cheating on me. What a dick."

"I'm so, so sorry," I whisper.

She just hangs her head and grabs a bottle of wine. "I need a drink, you?"

"No, thanks."

"Oh, c'mon, don't let me drown my sorrows alone."

"Okay, sure," I cave. I need to be a good friend.

She pours us two glasses, and immediately downs hers.

Then she pours herself another.

"I really thought that we were...in love. I mean, I really thought that he cared about me."

"Did he say anything?"

"Eh, the usual bullshit. It was a mistake. He still loves me. He just met her at a bar and it means nothing," Julie says, rolling her eyes. "But it's only seven at night. And they had already done it. So, either they met for an early bird special or...he knew her already. Either way, it doesn't fucking matter. He betrayed me."

I wrap my arms around her as she sobs into my shoulder.

My heart goes out to her and I try to think of something to say that will make everything better.

"I'm here for you," I whisper as she pulls away from me. Julie isn't the type to cry much and she quickly wipes her tears.

"This is stupid. I can do so much better than him anyway."

"Yes, you can."

"I deserve nothing but the best."

"Yes, you do," I agree.

"Okay, so let's go find someone."

"What?" I'm taken aback.

"I want to go out. I want to meet someone hotter, richer, and nicer than he is and I want to fuck him in Logan's bed."

"Julie...you're just angry. Why don't you just take it easy tonight?"

"No. I need to get revenge. He thinks he can cheat on me and get away with it? Well, I'll show him."

I need to calm her down.

I take her hand and pull her down on the couch next to me.

"Julie, you shouldn't have to sleep with a stranger just to settle some score."

"No, you're wrong. I'm not settling a score. I'm just acting like any other free woman would." She gets up and goes to the master bedroom.

"Where are you going?"

"To get ready."

I shake my head, trying to decide what to do.

I really don't want to go out with her, but she really shouldn't go out alone either.

"Are you sure you don't want to think about this some more? Sleep on it?"

She spins around in her swivel chair in front of the vanity. "I do need to think about it. And I do my best thinking in a club where the music is blaring."

CHAPTER 23 - HARLEY

THE NEXT DAY...

The following morning, I feel the way I usually feel after I go partying with Julie. Like an underpaid babysitter with a migraine.

Unfortunately, I am not successful in getting her to stay and I couldn't very well let her go out in that condition by herself.

So, I tag along, nursing the same drink all night.

I dance a little until my headache starts to build and then I find a dark corner and just hang out there watching her dance with every guy who takes an interest, and some who don't.

She doesn't get her fill until early into the next morning but, luckily, she drinks too much and is such a sloppy drunk that no one takes her up on her offer to spend the night.

I coax her into a cab after she refuses to take the subway, and we make it back home in one piece.

I'm so busy taking care of her that I don't spend much time worrying about the person driving us home.

Despite my best efforts, she throws up in the elevator and on Logan's doormat.

The second instance makes her laugh maniacally and even gives me a chuckle until I realize that I have go back and clean that up.

Logan won't be back for a bit, but there's a nice old lady who lives across the hall who shouldn't see something that gross on her way to walk her poodle.

After holding Julie's hair as she vomits into the toilet, and then helping her into bed, I clean.

"Fuck you, Logan," I say under my breath.

If he hadn't done that, I would be in bed right now getting my eight hours.

But instead I'm here, still in my club attire, scrubbing my friend's vomit off his toilet and front mat at four in the morning.

I SLEEP in late since Jackson texts and says he has a

lot of work to deal with today and can't see me until later.

When I finally do wake up around eleven, I'm awoken by Julie's loud voice and incessant cursing.

I know who she's talking to even before I leave my bed.

They got into another fight, but this time it's on the phone instead of Skype.

When I walk out, I see Julie pacing around the living room, gesticulating wildly as if Logan is here to see it.

It's hard to make out most of the words through the half sobs and screams, but I get the gist.

He cheated on her and she's angry.

I decide to give them some privacy and take my tea into my room.

Just as I open my computer, Julie slams the door open and flies in. Her eyes are wide and bloodshot, her hair is a mess, and her face has remnants of last night's makeup.

"We broke up."

I immediately get up and wrap my arms around her. She collapses on top of me and we both land on the bed.

"What happened?" I ask, propping her up.

Her body is limp and shaking with tears running down her face.

I move some of her hair out of the way, but it just drops back in.

"I dumped his cheating ass," she announces through her sobs.

"That was the right thing to do."

She takes a deep breath and then sobs, "No, it wasn't."

"Yes, it was. It was the right thing to do."

"I miss him."

"I know you do, honey. But that will pass."

"When?"

"It will take some time."

I continue to hold her as we talk.

She tells me about his secret texts and the other girls she saw him in pictures with on social media.

He always insisted that she had nothing to worry about and she trusted him.

Though the texts should've been a red flag, it really feels like this whole thing took her completely by surprise.

Julie wasn't like some of the other girls in our suite in college.

She was never really interested in steady boyfriends and was always the one to play the field.

That is until Logan came along.

Oh, I could just kill him.

Now, she's going to think that there's no point in ever trusting a man again and go back to her one-night stands.

Not that there's anything particularly wrong with that; she is a free woman in her twenties and if she wants to have sex with half of Manhattan that's her right.

But I also know that there's something wonderful about having that one person to turn to when life gets really shitty.

And dating one guy after another doesn't get you there.

"It's going to be okay, sweetie," I say over and over again as she sobs into my shoulder.

But I don't believe those words anymore than she does.

"I just can't believe that he would do that to me. Well, let me tell you, he is the first and last guy that ever does this to me."

"Julie, you are upset right now, but that doesn't mean that you can't trust the right man when he comes along."

"Oh, hell no." She shakes her head. "I don't need that kind of pain. I'm not falling for that again."

"Not everyone is a cheater."

She finally pulls away and looks directly at me.

"You better check Jackson's phone."

"Why?"

"Because... he's a guy. And not just a guy, he's loaded. And what would be the point of having all that money if you couldn't flaunt it to all the hotties out there?"

I don't want to get into this with her now, given that she's in such a fragile state, but she couldn't be more wrong. Jackson isn't like that at all.

A few minutes later, her tears seem to slow down a bit. She wipes her eyes with her palms and looks up at me.

"We can't stay here anymore."

Oh, shit.

CHAPTER 24 - HARLEY

CHANGES...

Somehow, it had completely slipped my mind that I have a very serious problem if I can't stay at Julie's house.

Parker Huntington is out of jail and even though I have a restraining order against him, that doesn't mean that he won't come looking for me.

That's the whole reason why I was even staying in their apartment with Julie while Logan was away on business.

"I guess it's my turn to ask you for a favor," Julie says.

I give her a slight nod, only half listening.

"Oh, c'mon, don't tell me you want me to beg?"

"What?"

TANGLED UP IN PAIN

"Fine, fine. Can I move back into our place?"

"Yes, of course! You don't even have to ask."

She lets out a sigh of relief.

"It's not as nice as this one, though," I say, looking around Logan's massive two-bedroom. "And it's not in as nice of an area."

She laughs. "But it has you there!"

I nod, yeah, for now.

"What? What's wrong?"

"Well, remember why you made me come here?"

"Oh, shit, of course!" She hits herself on her forehead with her palm. "No, you shouldn't go back there until his court case."

I shrug. "I think it's my only choice."

"What about Jackson? Doesn't he have that ridiculous mansion? I bet that if you moved in there, he wouldn't even notice it."

I laugh. She is more right than she can possibly know.

"I don't know if I can ask him. He's going through a lot of his own shit right now."

She nods. "Well, I'm happy for you to stay with me. I need some girl time."

"Me, too."

* * *

LOGAN DOESN'T GET BACK for a few more days, but
Julie doesn't want to stay there anymore.

We decide to move back the following day. Julie
packs a few things and I pack my bag from
Montana.

Since she moved all of her stuff over, it will take
her a few trips to bring it all back.

Personally, I don't see why we have to rush back
to our studio so soon, especially since Logan is still
away, but I don't argue.

The only reason I'm here in the first place is
because Julie extended me an invitation.

"Wow, this place is small!" she says, stepping
back into our place. "We have to get ourselves a two
bedroom."

I laugh. "Yeah, right. I can barely afford the rent
on this place."

After unpacking my stuff, I plop on my bed and
look at my phone.

Why hasn't he called?

Or texted?

He was supposed to last night, but he didn't.

I didn't message him either, mainly out of spite.

I mean, I know that he's going through a lot right
now, but so am I.

Finally, I decide to take my life into my own

hands and promise myself that I will call him if he doesn't contact me by three.

I call him at noon.

"Oh, hey, what's up?" His voice sounds detached and somewhere else.

"Just wanted to see how things are going over there."

"Um...okay. Busy."

"Oh, really?"

"Yeah, I'm trying to gather all of this paperwork to figure out exactly how much Swanson took from me. You know for the prosecutors."

"You've talked to them already."

"Of course."

The conversation doesn't get any better after that. Most of his answers are terse and one word in length.

After a few moments, I give up and say that I have to go.

But before he hangs up, he does remind me about the winter masquerade ball at Woodward's in the Hamptons on Friday night.

He asks if I want him to send a stylist again with a selection of outfits and I say yes.

It was nice not going to a store and trying on whatever they have.

Besides, for that event, I will need a very special dress, not one that I can afford to pay for myself.

* * *

THE STYLIST ARRIVES at our apartment two days later.

The place would seem a lot bigger without four people crammed into it, but Julie refuses to leave.

Fashion is something of a passion of hers.

Her eyes tint over with glee at the sight of just regular dresses at Nordstrom, let alone designer gowns like the ones that Mo arrives with.

Mo is a big woman with long eyelashes and a shaved head.

Her assistant is a mousy looking man with equally long eyelashes and perfectly groomed eyebrows.

They make themselves comfortable immediately and start laying out the outfits.

I try on the first dress, an A-line scoop neck organza ivory gown, which makes feel like a movie star.

I can't help but twirl around, looking at myself in Mo's large floor-length mirror that her assistant lugged up all those flights.

The second one is equally stunning.

It's a long-sleeve silk twill baroque-print midi dress.

But it's a bit unconventional and, as much as I want to wear long sleeves since I'm almost always cold, I decide to pass on it.

Two more dresses down and the first one I tried on is the one to beat.

"I think I'm just going to go with the first one. It feels like it's the best fit for this event."

Once I say that, Mo doesn't push anymore dresses on me.

Instead, she opens her large suitcase and starts to pull out boxes of shoes.

I take a deep breath, sit down on the edge of my bed, and start trying on shoes.

All are exquisitely beautiful and impractical.

Mo shows me the ones that go well with the dress I chose and out of those I go with the one that's the most comfortable.

"Now, you have to promise me that you're going to practice walking in those heels before the big day. At least an hour or two a day," Mo says.

"An hour a day!" I gasp.

"Harley isn't much for heels."

Now, it's Mo's turn to gasp. "Heels make the woman."

"Well, what does that say about me then?" I shrug.

"Oh, honey." Mo wraps her arms around me and gives me a big bear of a hug.

CHAPTER 25 - HARLEY

WHEN WE GO OUT TO DINNER...

The following night, Julie and I decide to go to our favorite restaurant.

It's a great little Indian place, right around the corner.

We arrive around seven and are surprised to find the place almost entirely to ourselves.

While this is usually a sign that something's wrong with the place, on this particular day we know we just hit the jackpot.

This place is never empty.

Just as we order our drinks and some appetizers, the flood gates open and people start to pile in.

"So, what's going on with you and Jackson?"

This is the first time she's asked me about him

since her breakup and I appreciate her taking an interest.

The truth is that nothing really is going on and that's what's making me so antsy.

We had this beautiful trip to Montana, in terms of how close it brought us, not what happened there with my family, and then nothing.

"He's sort of shutting me out. We've barely spoken two words to each other since the news about Swanson came out."

"Well, I'm sure that he's just busy dealing with all of that."

"He is. I know he is. We exchange texts a few times a day and talk on the phone a bit, but he's not really there, you know? He keeps saying that he wants to see me, but he can't right now."

"Why?" Julie asks, taking a bite of her naan.

"He is taking a lot of meetings with lawyers and prosecutors and they're all going over the paperwork that he received from Swanson over the years."

As I tell Julie what has been going on, I hear myself from the outside looking in and I realize how selfish and self-centered I sound.

Here he is trying to deal with losing his entire fortune while I'm complaining about him not giving me enough attention.

"So, are you still working for him?"

"Sort of. I mean, yes, I am. But I'm doing something different than I did that one day. I'm not his personal assistant anymore."

"Oh, yeah?" Julie raises her eyebrows with a look of glee in her eyes. "What do you mean, something different? Like sex different?"

I laugh and shake my head. "No. That stuff I do for free and I'm keeping it that way."

"Okay, what?"

"He knows that I really like to write so he's paying me to do that. To work on my novel."

"Wow, that's generous."

"Yeah, it is."

"Well, you better take your sweet time writing that sucker."

"I'm actually about halfway done," I say, looking away. Julie shakes her head.

"How do you live in this world, Harley? I mean, really?"

I shrug. "I just got so excited by the prospect of publishing it myself and him supporting my writing, and not just financially, that I couldn't stop writing. It's all I think about now."

* * *

After we finish our dinner, we decide to walk home.

I haven't taken a walk in I have no idea how long and it feels good to just be outside in the fresh air for once.

My boots make a loud clicking sound as they collide with the pavement.

Julie walks to a completely different rhythm so at first I don't hear those other footsteps behind us.

Until we turn onto a quieter street and they are impossible to not hear.

"What is that?" I ask.

Julie shrugs and I look behind me.

Somewhere in the distance the figure of a man disappears into one of the buildings.

It's not him.

It's not him, I say to myself, trying to convince myself that it's not Parker Huntington.

He wouldn't violate his restraining order to follow me here.

But of course he has in the past, and I know that he's fully capable of doing just about anything.

I take Julie by the arm and speed up our pace.

But the footsteps persist.

They stay behind, and don't get too close, but he keeps following us.

"Go away!" I say when I've finally had enough of the fear. "Don't follow me!"

I stop for a moment and wait, but then Julie pulls me away and into our building.

She makes sure that the door locks behind her before turning to face me.

"Are you crazy? Why are you baiting him?"

"Because I've had enough of that asshole. I've had enough of being scared and of worrying about seeing him again."

"I know you have, but he tried to actually hurt you before. You need to be more careful."

I don't know if it's just the couple of drinks of liquid courage that are coursing through my veins or if I am suddenly a lot less afraid of him.

Either way, I'm done putting up with his shit.

CHAPTER 26 - HARLEY

WHEN HE'S HERE...

The mask is white with long feathers around the eyes and sparkles and glitter everywhere else.

When I hold it in my hand it looks both exotic and familiar. It feels light in my hands, and when I put it on my face, it gives my appearance a mysterious stranger sort of feel.

Rather than something straight out of a garden variety Halloween store, this mask looks like it's from a Venetian specialty store.

Jackson greets me at my door.

He is dressed in a tuxedo with a matte tie the color of charcoal.

The total absence of color brings out the blue in

his irises, only emphasized by the dark mane that falls to one side in large, luxurious waves.

The exquisite tux is perfectly tailored, hugging his wide shoulders and narrowing at his waist.

After running his gaze up and down my body, his eyes bore into mine.

His lips fall slightly apart before he utters a word. "You...take my breath away."

I blush and take a step closer to him.

Raising my chin up, I press my lips onto his.

"Hi, I'm her roommate Julie."

She's standing with her arm extended, waiting to shake his hand.

"I've heard a lot about you. It's a pleasure to meet you," Jackson says.

"Pleasure is all mine. You want to come in?"

My eyes get big like two saucers as I glare at Julie.

Why would she invite him in?

Our place is...so small and in such disarray.

"Unfortunately, we don't have much time," Jackson says. I let out a sigh of relief.

"But I'd love a quick tour."

My whole body recoils and clenches up.

As Julie welcomes him inside, I shake my head at her and mouth, what are you doing?

Julie smiles innocently back at me, mouthing back, what?

"That's my side over there. Sorry about the mess, but I'm just moving back in." Julie points to her bed covered in open suitcases and piles of clothes. Because Logan's apartment was already furnished she'd left all of her furniture including her bed, desk, bookcase, and chair.

My side is in a lot better shape.

Ever since I was a little girl, I've always liked a neat bed, so I rarely go a day without making it.

Luckily, the process of actually 'making' it isn't very complicated.

Without bothering with straightening out the sheet underneath, I just pull my plush gray comforter all the way to the headboard, stack the pillows vertically, placing the decorative one in front of the pillow-cased one and voila.

The comforter is thick enough to make the bed look well made without actually going through the process of doing it.

My little white desk is likewise pretty clear of papers and other debris entirely out of necessity.

It has only enough square space across to fit my laptop, a cup of tea, and a candle and if it were cluttered up with anything else, then I wouldn't have any space to work.

I don't have many papers, after my massive post-college purge, and I keep all of my journals and handwritten stuff in decorative boxes in my closet.

"She's kind of a neat freak," Julie points out.

"No, I'm not."

"Not when it comes to actually cleaning the toilet, but you do like things organized."

My mortification is now complete.

Instead of descending down the stairs like the process I felt like only a few moments ago when I first saw him at the door in his tuxedo, we are now discussing my ability or inability to clean a *toilet*.

I think I'm actually going to kill her.

"It's the only way I can ever find anything. I don't know how you find anything in there." I point to her bed.

"Eh, if I can't, I'll just go buy it," Julie jokes, tossing her hair over her shoulder in a dramatic way.

But she's only partly joking.

I've seen her do this on a number of occasions.

"Did she tell you about her minimalism kick?"

Jackson smiles, clearly amused.

"We have to go." I take him by the arm and try to push him toward the door.

But he doesn't budge.

"No, I want to hear."

Liking the attention, Julie continues, "Yeah, she read these books about how getting rid of stuff that you don't absolutely love will make you happy and then she went on this crusade to rid herself of practically everything."

"Not everything. Just stuff that I didn't care for."

"Is that why you only have three pairs of shoes in your closet?"

"I didn't like the other ones."

"What kind of self-respecting woman has only three pairs of shoes in her closet?" Julie asks Jackson.

He laughs, shrugging his shoulders.

"Okay, now, we really have to go."

Luckily, this time Jackson gives in and lets me usher him out of the door.

"It has been an absolute pleasure, Julie," he says, shaking her hand again.

Just before closing the door, and with Jackson's back to her, I whisper, "You suck."

"You're fine," Julie says with a big grin on her face. "Have fun, you two."

"I can't believe she told you all of that," I say, burying my face in my hands as we walk down the hallway.

"Oh, c'mon, she was just having fun."

"Yep, it's always good fun to embarrass someone."

"What was so embarrassing?"

"Just... telling you that I'm a neat freak and I got rid of all of my stuff."

It takes me a moment to put that into words, but as I say that I realize that's not really what I find the most shameful.

It's the fact that he saw our apartment.

"I guess I just wasn't ready for you to see my place," I mumble. "It's not exactly the Ritz."

"I wasn't expecting it to be."

I shrug.

Jackson stops walking and pulls me into his arms. "Harley, you have nothing to be ashamed of. You live on your own—"

"Well, I share a studio with a roommate."

He puts his finger on my lips.

"You pay your own bills. You are making your own way in a very expensive city. And your apartment is charming. The reason I wanted a tour was that I wanted to have an image of where you are when we are apart. And now, I can see you there, sitting at your desk. Sleeping on your bed. And now I do."

CHAPTER 27 - HARLEY

ABOUT THE CITY...

When we get outside, I expect Mr. Garbo to be waiting for us, but instead he presses a button on his keychain and a car's headlights flash and a pre-programmed sequence of exterior lighting welcomes us inside.

The emblem at the front has a large B with a pair of wings.

It has clean, super formed lines and a wide body that sits low to the ground.

Jackson opens the door for me, and when I take a seat, I'm illuminated by interior mood lighting.

I've never been inside a car that was anything like this.

Its beautiful trim has a natural grain of wood contrasting with a clean, minimalist black finish.

The center console is elongated and white with another sleek finish.

"What kind of car is this?" I ask as we fly down the street inside an almost soundless cabin.

"It's a Bentley Continental GT."

"Do you like cars?"

"No, not really. But this one is...magnificent."

"Thank you." He smiles.

"I like that Chagall painting you have hanging above your bed."

I found it at a thrift store awhile ago.

I remember I spent seventy-five dollars on it, seventy-five dollars that I didn't really have.

Its large and imposing and came with a decorative gold frame that seemed to fit it perfectly.

I debated whether I should buy it for about a week before actually making the commitment.

And I haven't regretted it since.

"Thank you, he's my favorite artist."

"The Bride and Groom of the Eiffel Tower." Jackson names the title of the painting.

"That's right. He painted it in 1939."

"What do you like about it?"

"The colors are really striking. Bright yellows, blues, and reds. Also, I love how the groom is facing the bride and there's a giant chicken behind them, you know, just because." I laugh. "Chagall wasn't much of a realist."

"And don't forget the goat playing the guitar."

"The violin or is it a viola?" I smile. "How can anyone forget that?"

As we talk, whatever tension existed between us seems to vanish completely.

I'm not sure if it ever really existed except in my own mind.

We are heading to the Hamptons, which is about a two-hour drive from Manhattan.

Just as I settle in for the drive, we make a turn into what looks like a large lot. It's pitch black, so I don't have great visibility.

"Where are we going?"

"We're taking a helicopter."

Jackson hands someone the keys to his car and helps me up into it.

To say it's a bit of a struggle in a gown would be an understatement. But once we take off, the view is well worth it.

Manhattan rises all around us, each building taller than the next.

Flying this high above the traffic makes everything a spectacle of lights.

I stare out of the window for the entire forty minutes it takes us to land.

Once we get to the Hamptons, we are greeted by another man with another car, this time a BMW.

The Hamptons are really a summer destination for the wealthy elite of Manhattan.

Though there are a number of locals who live here year-round, running businesses that cater to the tourists, there isn't the same slew of activity here in the winter as there is in the summer.

"Have you ever been here before?" Jackson asks as we make our way down an empty road.

"A few years ago, Julie and about ten other people pitched in to rent a small two-bedroom cottage nowhere near the beach and I ended up going home early because someone peed on my cot and the party got to be too much."

This makes him laugh.

"I'm sorry we haven't had much time to talk this week."

"It's okay, I understand."

"I've just been going through so much with this whole Swanson debacle."

I nod.

"But I miss you."

"I miss you, too."

We drive for a few moments in silence.

"You know, you can talk to me about anything, right?" I say. "You don't have to shut me out. You can tell me anything and your secrets will be safe with me."

"I don't really have any secrets."

"You know what I mean."

He takes a deep breath. I can see that this is a struggle for him.

"Minetta is losing a lot of money," he says after a moment. "Everyday. I thought it was going much better than it was, but I had a meeting with my CFO this week and things look bleak, to say the least. We've expanded too fast and our readership and engagement is way down. That means that our ad revenues are going down. We've decided to shut down two divisions of content that were performing the worst, but it's not enough to stop the bleeding. There are going to be layoffs within the company as well."

"I'm so sorry."

"I was planning on divesting from the Swanson fund if anything like this happened. I had invested a lot with him and then, according to the returns that he sent, I thought that money had really mushroomed into something quite substantial. But now that it's all a lie, I've lost what I put in as well. As far as the lawyers can tell, that is."

"What do you mean?"

"Well, it will take a long time for them to go through everyone's paperwork and figure out exactly how much I and all the other investors lost. But for now, I don't have access to any of that money, not even the original amount I invested."

"What are you going to do?" I ask.

"I have a few options, none of them really that good. I can sell the company, but given its current financial situation, it's not doing that well, so it won't fetch a good price. At least, not one that is appropriate to how well it has done in the past and how well I know it can do once it survives this cash-flow problem."

I nod. "And the other options?"

"I can try to make a deal with an investment bank to take it public and infuse it with cash on the open market. Unfortunately, because it is losing money now, it again won't get a good deal. And then, I'll have to answer to shareholders as well."

"That doesn't sound good."

He shakes his head no.

"My other option is to put my house on the market. It went up in price a bit, and if it sells for that price, then I will at least have some money to put back into the business."

He stares straight ahead as he speaks, saying everything in a matter-of-fact way.

His face is expressionless and blank, but I know that this is really hurting him inside.

He is losing everything that he worked for and built up from scratch.

"Where does Woodward fit in?" I ask.

CHAPTER 28 - HARLEY

WHEN THE MASKS GO ON...

Jackson looks over at me.

The one thing that isn't void of all expression and coldness are his eyes.

There's a desperation in them. Instead of the shrewd glare that they typically look at me with, I see cracks in the gaze.

Perhaps, even something resembling mist.

"I don't know where that puts Woodward," he says. "That's why we're here. If he's willing to invest at the terms we talked about before, then I'm all ears. I'm happy to do business with him. The problem is that I know that he knows that I'm going through some financial difficulties. He definitely knows about Swanson."

"But not how much you lost, right?"

"No, probably not. I can downplay that, but he'll know that it will give him some leverage."

I nod. The situation looks rather grave.

"What do you want me to do?" I ask as we pull up to a brightly lit mansion and a valet takes the car keys.

"Just be your normal charming self. He seemed to like you; maybe that's something I can use to my advantage."

I nod, never feeling like I've had more weight on my shoulders than I do at this moment.

I know that when Jackson said to be nice, he doesn't want me to flirt with Woodward, let alone do anything else beyond that, but I still feel like this deal is partly on me and my behavior.

We put on our masks and make our way through the sea of other people, also wearing masks.

All I see are gowns and tuxedos all around me.

No one has a face.

I thought that it would feel strange to not see anyone eye-to-eye, but it's actually quite refreshing.

I'm not a particularly outgoing person, being at these fancy events, I always feel a little bit uncomfortable and really out of place.

But with this mask on my face, I'm suddenly just one of the crowd.

I fit in. I'm one of the beautiful ladies who walk around with glasses of champagne making small talk with each other.

I don't stand out one bit.

"Thank you for coming. I know it's a bit of a trip." Our host comes up to me and places his hand on the small of my back.

I recoil at first but then quickly relax into it because it would be rude not to.

Elliot Woodward pulls his mask to his forehead as he bends over and gives me a peck on the cheek. I reciprocate but keep my mask firmly in place.

"You look absolutely stunning."

"Thank you, your party is...amazing."

"My team aims to please," he says and then shakes Jackson's hand.

They chat for a bit, about nothing in particular, and then Woodward excuses himself to make the rounds.

"Hosting duties await," he says. "But we will absolutely talk business tonight. Later, in private."

"I'm looking forward to it," Jackson says.

I watch his demeanor during their brief talk and I'm amazed by how self-assured and confident Jackson appears.

Whatever fears he has have been buried deep

inside and now he is simply the cool, calm, completely unfazed businessman that he was before.

Grabbing two new glasses of champagne, we start making our own rounds.

Jackson hasn't been seen in public much, but everyone here seems to know him and he knows everyone else.

He introduces them to me with poignant anecdotes, immediately charming them.

I try to match his casual friendliness by smiling a bit too much and being too eager to talk to just about every stranger he introduces me to.

After I've met and forgotten about twenty people's names, Jackson excuses himself to go to the restroom and I take a moment to step out onto the patio for a breath of fresh air.

"Excuse me, Ms. Burke? Harley Burke?" A flamingo of a woman on long legs and even longer torso approaches me.

"Yes, can I help you?"

"Will you come with me, please? Mr. Woodward would like a word with you."

"Me? Are you sure you aren't looking for Jackson?"

She smiles, shaking her head. "He asked specifically for you. Only you."

My heart jumps into my throat.

Me?

Why would he ask for me?

I follow her toward the back of the house, to the kitchen, and up the marble staircase.

There is no party here, and the walls are so thick that you can't even hear that there's a party going on downstairs.

"What does he want?"

"I'm not really sure."

After we reach a large wooden door with intricate carvings on the outside, the woman presses the doorbell and waits.

Maybe no one is here, I think joyfully, when no one responds for a moment.

But my hopes are quickly dashed.

"Come in," Elliot says after a moment.

He stands up when I walk in and leads me to the couch near the fireplace.

"Would you like anything to drink?" he asks, pouring himself a glass of whiskey.

I lift up the glass of champagne that I still have in my hand. "No, thank you."

"Thank you for coming, Harley. May I call you Harley?"

"Yes, of course." He takes a seat directly in front

of me in a large stuffed leather chair that makes a squeaking sound as he reclines into it.

"I have to be honest with you, I don't really understand why I'm here."

He puts his finger up at me and takes a whiff of his drink.

Then he slowly brings it up to his lips, taking a moment to swallow and enjoy his sip.

If he thinks that this is charming, then he must be delusional.

It annoys me that he's wasting my time making me watch him.

But I don't dare say a word.

I don't want to do anything to jeopardize Jackson's deal.

"Wow, that's good," he says, placing his arm on the armrest and then looking me up and down.

"I have a proposition for you, Harley."

Confused, I furrow my brows.

"What kind of proposition?"

CHAPTER 29 - HARLEY

IN HIS OFFICE...

I wait for answer, but then he suddenly changes the topic.

He gets up and starts pacing the room.

"What do you think about my party?" he asks.

I don't want to be rude, so I answer.

"It's really beautiful. I've never been here in the winter."

"Yes, I know. The Hamptons are pretty dead around this time of year. A lot of the locals really struggle to make ends meet. You know, no summer people with their big wallets to overspend on everything."

I nod.

It's amazing how he can sound both sympathetic and like a total rich asshole at the same time.

"There aren't too many fun things to do around here this time of year. Christmas is over and it's not spring yet, so I thought, what the hell? Why not do something lavish to break up this horrible winter?"

"Well, you certainly succeeded." I take another sip of my champagne and wait for him to tell me why he really brought me here.

He walks closer to me, but instead of sitting down across from me, he takes a seat right next to me.

He's so close that I actually scoot a little away from him, but there's nowhere to really go since I'm on the edge of the couch.

Elliot places his arm around the back of the couch and moves a little bit closer.

"Why did you bring me here?"

He licks his lips before answering.

"I was just wondering exactly how interested you are in me saving your friend's company?"

My heart sinks to the pit of my stomach.

All the blood seems to drain away from my face and I freeze.

"What do you mean?"

"Well, you know." He places his hand on my knee.

Before I can remove it, it's traveling up my leg.

"What are you doing?" I push my hand against his. He exhales and sits back against the couch.

"I thought we had a bit of a connection," he says.

"Just because I was nice to you?"

"Yeah," he says nonchalantly.

"I'm with Jackson."

"Why do you want to have anything to do with that hermit? He hasn't left the house in ages and he probably doesn't even know how to fuck properly."

"You don't know anything about him," I hiss and rise to my feet.

"Maybe. Maybe not. But I do know something about *you*," he says, standing up as well.

I narrow my eyes.

"You are an escort. Men pay you money, good money, for you to do bad things to them. Well, whatever Jackson is paying you, I'll double it."

I shake my head in disgust.

"I am *not* an escort."

"Really? What about your blog?"

Saying that word, it's as if he had hit the side of my head with a bag of rocks.

"Oh, you didn't think that I would know. Well, surprise!" His voice is coarse and taunting. He is enjoying this. A lot.

I've had enough.

Without another word, I head straight toward the door.

But he blocks me.

Shivers run down my spine as I have a flashback to being in that car with the doors locked.

He pulls my hair back and presses his mouth onto mine.

I try to push him away, but he is holding me too tightly.

So, I do the only thing that comes to mind.

I bite down on his lower lip as hard as I can.

"You bitch!" he yells, holding onto his bleeding mouth.

I grab the door and run out.

From the main stairwell, I scan the room for Jackson but I can't pick him out of the crowd.

Everyone is in masks and he could be any of the dark haired men in tuxedos.

Shit.

My heart is racing.

I need to get out of this house as soon as possible.

Instead of searching for him and wasting time, I run out of the front door and past the valets.

I don't stop until I reach the end of the driveway.

There, I hide behind the bushes on the other side, and with trembling hands, pull out my phone.

I dial his number.

He doesn't respond, so I start to type.

Still shaken by what just happened, my mind isn't thinking clearly.

It takes me a couple of tries to get the words right.

CHAPTER 30 - JACKSON

WHEN I LOOK FOR HER...

hen I come back from the bathroom, I don't see her anywhere.

Granted, it's hard to pick her out of the crowd just by her hair or face, but I walk around the room and look for her gown.

Still, nowhere to be found.

A few people from the Barnes Foundation come over and we chitchat for awhile.

It doesn't take long for the conversation to turn to Swanson and for them to complain that they have lost a significant amount of their funds in the fraud.

I can see that they aren't simply asking me to sympathize with them but are doing everything besides coming right out and asking me for a donation.

But I play dumb and eventually, disappointed, they excuse themselves.

As I make another circle around the room, I don't spot Harley, but I do see Woodward. He's getting a drink at the bar and there's no one talking to him.

I think this is as good a time as ever to have this conversation.

"Hey, I just wanted to thank you for inviting me again." When he turns around, I see a large cut on his lip.

"Is everything alright?"

"Couldn't be better," he says sarcastically. "Actually, why don't we go and have that private chat right now?"

I follow him out onto the terrace, overlooking his expansive garden styled to look like the gardens of Versailles.

"So, what happened to your lip?"

"Eh, it's nothing."

I don't press and instead pivot to our previous conversation.

I again review all the positive aspects of our business model and plan, just like I did before.

He listens carefully as I make my case, nodding only occasionally.

It's hard to tell how it's going because he is very difficult to read.

Suddenly, he interrupts me.

"That all sounds good. And you've said all of those things before."

"Okay...so, what else would you like to know?"

He leans on the railing, looking out into the distance.

"You know, a lot of people don't like the Hamptons in the winter. They flew from this place between Memorial Day and Labor Day. This place that they love so much during the summers, they completely forget in the winters."

I nod. "It is quiet."

"Yes! That's exactly what it is," he says, pointing his finger at me in exclamation. "I think that's what appeals to me about it. Sometimes, I come here on the weekends just to get away. You know, the city can be awfully noisy."

"I agree. I also enjoy peace and quiet."

"Do you have a summer house here?"

"No, I don't."

"Eh, not everyone does. I sometimes think I'm a fool for not renting. I mean, why pay a mortgage all year for something you mainly use in the summer."

I nod in agreement.

It's hard to put into words, but I have a feeling that something is wrong. Like he's saying this just to goad me.

But I don't trust it.

You don't know him, I say to myself.

Maybe this is his way of making friends.

"So...you like the peace and quiet, too, huh?"

"Yes."

He turns to face me, looks directly into my eyes, and asks, "Is that why you holed up in your mansion for four years without setting foot outside?"

His tone is rude.

Severe.

He doesn't even try to pretend like he's making a joke.

I take a deep breath.

That aspect of my life wasn't exactly public knowledge, but I've read the gossip magazines and I've heard the rumors.

"I don't know what you're talking about," I say without blinking or pausing for a moment to think.

"Hmm." He chuckles. "That's what I've heard."

"Your sources must be confused."

"My sources are never confused."

We glare into each other's eyes, neither one looking away first.

Finally, he caves and pulls away.

"Well, anyway, if you were a bit of a recluse then that would explain it then."

"Explain what?"

"Why you brought a known whore to my party."

His words take me by surprise.

"What the hell are you talking about?"

"Harley, your date? She's an escort. Don't get me wrong, I don't frown on sex work that much. I mean, I've been known to use one or two of them in my day. But to bring her to my party? When you were trying to raise investments? I mean, c'mon? Are you serious?"

"Are you serious? She's not an escort."

"Prostitute, lady of the night. Whatever you want to call her."

"She's not one of those things."

"Oh." He raises his eyebrows. "You don't know, do you? About the blog?"

I clench my jaw.

"I know about the fucking blog. And it's all fiction."

"Yeah, right." He rolls his eyes. "And she was a

virgin when she met you. C'mon, man, listen to yourself."

I take a deep breath. Blood running through my veins starts to simmer and come to a boil.

"She's not an escort and let's leave it at that," I say, glaring at him. "Now, if you don't want to talk about what we came here to discuss then I'll be going."

"Fine," he says. "Okay, let's discuss what you came to discuss. You are running a failing company that is in desperate need of a big cash infusion just to keep its doors open next month. You have lost, what, half a billion dollars in Swanson's Ponzie scheme, definitely enough to knock you off that Forbes List and make it a bit difficult to use your personal wealth to prop up your company. You are desperate. So desperate, in fact, that you put out feelers with your realtor to see if anyone is interested in buying your ridiculously overpriced *old* house, but no one is biting yet, are they?"

I clench my jaw.

He is a lot more informed than I thought that he would be.

In fact, a bit too informed. It's almost as if someone has been feeding him private information from the inside.

"So, I gather you're not interested?" I ask coolly.

"No. Not yet. What I am interested in is buying your company when it declares bankruptcy for pennies on the dollar. What I am interested in is taking your friend, Harley, out on a proper date, without first paying her a grand, and fucking her sideways."

I make a fist and punch him squarely in his mouth.

"What the —" he starts to say, cradling his face.

So, I punch him again.

The second blow knocks him off his feet and he falls, stunned to the floor.

AFTERMATH...

"*Y*ou're going to pay for this!" Woodward yells at me as I walk out from the terrace and head toward the front door.

I know that security is on its way here, and I don't need any special handling.

As soon as I'm outside, I realize that Harley is still inside.

I pick up my phone, ready to warn her and see the messages that I've missed.

The valet hands me my keys and I take off.

I can't believe that she's walking back, I shake my head.

Back where?

I never booked a hotel.

I screech out of the front gate and turn right, following the directions on her text.

I dial her phone over and over again, but it goes straight to voice mail.

"C'mon, Harley, where are you?" As I drive down the empty two-lane highway, which is illuminated only by headlights and the moon above, I slow down a bit.

I want to make sure that I don't miss her and that I don't, God forbid, hit her.

Walking along these winding roads late at night is highly dangerous and my current state is a mix of anger and worry over where she is.

About two miles away from the house, I finally spot her.

The wind picks up her gown and tosses it haphazardly around her.

She is walking barefoot, holding her heels in one hand.

I beep the horn a few times as I approach.

Once I pull over next to her, she cautiously approaches the car and looks in.

"Jackson!" Harley climbs in and gives me a big hug.

She doesn't have a coat and, wrapped only in her large shawl, she is shivering.

"What happened?" I ask.

She puts her hands next to the heaters.

When she opens her mouth, all I hear is the chatter of her teeth.

"I couldn't find you anywhere."

"I know, I couldn't find you either," I say.

"I'm so, so sorry. I really fucked things up."

"That can't possibly be true given how much I fucked things up," I say.

"What do you mean?"

"You first."

She takes a deep breath and tells me how Woodward cornered her and came on to her.

"So, you were the one who gave him that thick lip?" I ask, starting to laugh.

"Yes...what's so funny?"

"Well, let's just say that we really did a number on him tonight. I punched him. Twice."

Her mouth falls open as I tell my story.

Whatever inkling of regret I'd started to feel right after I punched him over overreacting and letting him get the best of me, vanish completely.

In fact, the pendulum swings the other way completely.

Not only do I feel completely justified for doing

what I did, but I sort of wish that I'd hurt him a little more.

The flight and the drive back is uneventful and as soon as we get back into the Bentley, I ask her if she wants to come sleep over at my place.

"I thought that you would never ask," Harley says with a little smile on her face.

* * *

FINALLY, we are in my bedroom.

It has been way too long since I've peeled her clothes off her and made her mine.

I bring her closer to me, by holding onto the small of her back.

She is still shivering, only now she's shivering at my touch.

She closes her eyes to fight off the surge of arousal that I can feel is coursing through her veins.

I inhale the scent from the top of her head - something flowery with a mix of lavender.

It's absolutely intoxicating.

Her small frame, which was ice cold only a few moments before, is now starting to radiate some of my heat.

I want to rip off her clothes and toss her on the

bed, but I suppress the wild desire within me for as long as possible.

For things are better when you have to wait.

I run my fingers down the outside of her arms as they rest by her sides.

As soon as I reach her hands, she raises them up and buries them in my hair.

My body is starting to respond to hers and I can't help but press myself harder against her.

I unzip the back of her dress and let it slide off her body.

I press my lips to her neck and follow its curve down to her rising breasts.

"I love you," I whisper.

"I love you, too."

"You know you can tell me anything, right?" I say as my tongue makes its way down to her navel.

"Yes, of course," she moans.

"Good."

"Why?"

"Just...never mind." I decide not to pursue this.

Why did I even bring this up?

But I've caught Harley's attention and she stops me and pulls me back up to my feet.

"What are you talking about?" she asks.

I shake my head.

"C'mon...you can tell me anything, too, remember?"

I take a deep breath.

"It's stupid."

"Tell me anyway."

"Okay...well, I just wanted you to know that I won't get mad if that stuff about you being an escort was true."

"What?" She takes a step back from me and whatever uneasiness I felt about talking about this only a few minutes ago confirms my worst fears.

"You think I was an escort? You think I lied to you about doing that?"

"No, no...I don't know what to think. I just wanted to tell you that I wouldn't get mad if you were."

"Well, I'm mad because you would even think something like that."

"Look, you wrote that whole blog about it...of course, it's possible that you would lie to me."

"Fuck you," she says, grabbing her dress.

"Oh, c'mon, Harley, don't be like that. Don't let this ruin our night."

"Ruin our night? It's going to do a lot more than that! You talk to that asshole Woodward one time and you believe him over me? Well, you can just go fuck yourself then, Jackson."

"I do believe you," I say, running after her.

She makes her way quickly down the stairs, grabs her shawl off the dining room table, and puts on her heels.

"I do believe you," I repeat myself.

"No, you don't. If you did, then you wouldn't have said that. I told you the truth back there. I told you I was a virgin, which I was. Do you know how embarrassing it is to be a twenty-something virgin in New York City? The city where everyone fucks on the first date? It would've been easier for me to tell you I was an escort than what I really was. And now...now you're questioning me? You think I'm lying?"

"No, I don't."

"But you did. You doubted me. And that's...I can't, Jackson."

I walk up to her and grab her arm to try to get her to stay, but she pulls away and slams the front door behind her.

CHAPTER 32 - HARLEY

AFTERMATH...

The next three days are a blur.

After walking around the Hamptons and running out of Jackson's house in a light dress and a shawl, I inevitably get the flu.

My head is pounding and my nose is runny.

I have a high temperature and I can't even open my eyes without them tearing up.

I lie in bed for three full days and Julie brings me soup and crackers.

Finally, on the fourth day, I'm feeling good enough to actually get up and heat up my own soup in the microwave.

Since we live in a studio, Julie and I both wear masks to keep the germs to my side of the room.

It doesn't bother me much since I spend most of the time sleeping.

Luckily, by the weekend I'm feeling much better and Julie doesn't catch anything from me.

"He keeps calling you." Julie points to my phone as it vibrates again for what is the third time today.

I shrug.

"He called me, too."

"He did? What did you say?"

"I told him you were sick and that you didn't want to talk to him."

As I slurp my soup, sitting against the headboard, Julie curls up next to me. "Are you sure you don't want to call him back? He seems really sorry."

"I just can't believe that he thought I was actually lying about something like that."

"Oh, c'mon, everybody lies."

"I wouldn't."

"Is it really that outrageous though? I mean, you did write that sexy blog that got all those views."

I shake my head. "I told him the truth and he didn't believe me. He believed that scumbag Woodward over me."

"He was just double-checking," she argues his case.

"Are you his lawyer or something?"

"No, I just don't want you to mess this good thing up over something so...dumb."

"It's not dumb. It's just proof of what he really thinks about me."

She starts to say something in return, but I stop her.

"I don't want to talk about this anymore."

As the days pass, his calls get less and less frequent.

I don't answer any of them and I don't reply to any of his texts.

Occasionally, when I'm lying awake late at night I wonder if I'm being too rigid, but then Woodward's face comes into my mind.

Jackson said the same vile thing to me as Woodward did and I just can't get over it.

No matter how many times he apologizes.

What hurts me the most is that he didn't believe me.

The morning that Julie starts her second job as a temporary assistant at a law firm, it dawns on me that along with a boyfriend I also dumped a really great job that paid me to write a novel.

Shit.

I open my laptop and stare at the list of possible content articles to write, each one looking less appealing than the one before.

Given that I'm not getting any work done anyway, I decide to put it away for today.

My thoughts keep drifting back to Jackson and how much I miss him.

So, I focus my attention on the only thing I can, my novel.

Even though Jackson is no longer paying me, the urge to keep writing continues to burn.

So, I click on my novel and start writing.

It takes me a bit to remember where I was and what was happening, but once I start, the story seems to come so fast I can barely keep up with it.

Two pages later, my hands starts to cramp up, but I don't stop until I have ten full pages.

I take a break and make myself a cup of tea and then look up the podcasts that Jackson had mentioned about self-publishing.

There're actually a lot of them with many good reviews.

I put one on and listen.

The host interviews an author of historical romances, who has been rejected by thirty traditional publishers and then turned to self-publishing.

She talks about the desperation she felt when she published her first book, the desperation to sell even one book.

But much to her surprise, readers started discovering her books and downloading them like crazy.

Of course, some of her initial success had to do with beginner's luck, and her second book didn't sell as many copies until she researched and planned out a good marketing strategy, which relied heavily on social media advertising.

Now, she sells about fifty thousand books a year, "more than what she would've ever sold through any publisher."

I sit, listening to her talk in amazement.

As soon as the episode is done, I turn back to my laptop and continue writing.

CHAPTER 33 - JACKSON

WHEN SHE GHOSTS ME...

I keep trying her phone without much success. I keep texting her, but again I hear nothing.

At first I thought that I would be able to get through eventually, but now I'm starting to think that this isn't just a fight and that she's actually not interested in seeing me anymore.

A couple of times, I go over to her place and ring the doorbell. No one answers for a long time, until they do.

It's Julie and she tells me that Harley has no interest in talking to me.

My world turns to black.

I miss her and I want her, and I can't have her.

I've made the terrible mistake of bringing that up and now she has shut me out of her life completely.

I feel like such a fool, I also get angry. I didn't do anything that terrible. I just posed a question.

I wasn't questioning her.

I was just leaving the field open for her to admit the truth in case she hadn't before.

My jaw clenches from the rage that's boiling up within me.

I'm angry at Woodward, I'm angry at Harley.

But mostly, I'm angry at myself.

I let him get to me.

I let him and his vile thought intrude on my life.

And now...the one good thing I had in it is gone.

If she won't answer my calls and she won't answer my texts or the door, and the emails I send to her go unanswered, maybe she'll at least read my letters.

I pick up a pen and paper and start the first letter.

EVEN THOUGH THE market for my particular property doesn't look promising, I give the realtor the okay to list it for sale.

It's priced low for a quick sale, and if this goes through then I won't make much more than a million dollars in profit.

That's not that much on a property that cost me thirty.

But at least I won't have a large mortgage hanging over my head and it will give me some cash flow to deal with the Minetta situation.

After the photographer comes through, the realtor hosts the first open house, and I take the Bentley for a drive.

I go nowhere in particular, just north. I drive all the way to North Riverdale before I turn around and head back to Manhattan.

Once I'm back in town, I again circle around and stop by Harley's place.

Again, she refuses to meet with me.

Again, I promise myself that I'm going to give up, but I know that I won't.

I come back home just after the open house is complete.

"Uh oh," I say when I see the realtor's disappointing look. "That bad?"

"No, not at all." He shakes his head and puts on a brave face. I roll my eyes.

"It will pick up. It was just a bad day."

"Okay," I say, not really believing his bullshit.

But what choice do I have?

When he packs up his stuff and leaves, I plop on the couch and make myself comfortable in front of the television.

I watch a few episodes of whatever, lost in a mindless stupor.

The only thing that gets me off the couch is the delivery guy who shows up with food from my favorite Indian place.

Then, suddenly, around nine that evening the doorbell rings.

I'm not expecting anyone and I jump up excited.

It's her.

It has to be her.

I glance at myself in the mirror and straighten out my hair.

The doorbell rings again.

There's no time to change clothes; these sweats will just have to do.

I open the door with a big wide smile on my face.

It quickly evaporates once I see who is on the other side.

"Expecting someone else?"

"Hoping for someone else," I say without missing a beat.

"Oh, c'mon, don't be like that." She pushes right past me and walks into the foyer.

"Yes, please come in," I say sarcastically.

"I will, thank you." She waves her hand and walks directly to the kitchen.

She grabs a glass from the cupboard and helps herself to some water from the tap.

"Don't forget, this is my house as well."

"Was," I correct her.

She spins on her high heeled boots to face me.

Pushing her sandy blond hair up with one hand, she takes off her dark sunglasses.

That's when I see it.

Her left eye is entirely black and blue.

"Oh, shit, what happened?"

She opens the freezer and grabs a bag of peas.

Pressing them lightly to her face, she gives me a shrug.

Her scarf slides off her perfectly tailored jacket from Saks Fifth Avenue, no doubt, and exposes more bruises.

"Aurora, what happened?"

"Just a side effect of being married to a European royal."

"This is not funny."

"It's not the first time."

"Why are you still with him?"

"Because he buys me diamonds, cars, and houses and I get to have dinner with the Queen," she says with her usual dry sense of humor. "Because I love him, you idiot."

I stare at her, shaking my head.

"Aren't you going to offer to take my coat?"

"Can I take your coat?" I ask, absentmindedly.

She rolls her eyes and walks back out of the front door.

"Ah, it's finally here!" she says, coming back with a suitcase.

I suddenly snap out of my trance. "Aurora, what are you doing?"

"I'm staying here."

"No, you're not."

"This house is mine."

"No, it's not."

"I helped you pay for it behind my husband's back. So, letting me stay here is the least you can do."

It's more of a statement than a request, but I'm used to her crude manners.

Confronting her head-on isn't always the best approach.

"Why don't you go stay at a hotel?"

"I want to be near family," she says in that whimsical way of hers.

"I'm not your family."

"Jackson, we got divorced. That doesn't mean we ever stopped being family."

I take a deep breath and follow her to the guest room on the first floor.

This has always been one of her favorite rooms.

I place her suitcase by the door.

"Fine, but you can't stay long."

Finally, her nonchalant demeanor changes and she whispers, "Thank you."

CHAPTER 34 - JACKSON

SURPRISE...

*R*unning her long manicured fingernails along the quartz countertop of the kitchen island, Aurora looks around the room.

She is dressed in a short black dress with long black sleeves, which ties in the front.

Dark charcoal leggings and matching ankle boots.

Her Louis Vuitton purse lays on the dining room table while her Louis Vuitton suitcase is tucked away in one of the downstairs guest rooms.

How the hell did this happen?

Only half an hour ago, I went to the door thinking that Harley had finally forgiven me.

And now...my ex-wife is shacking up with me.

As she looks around, she finishes her glass of water and quickly pours herself another.

"Particularly thirsty?" I ask.

She pulls out her phone and enters something into an app.

"I'm tracking my water intake now. I'm aiming for one and a half to two gallons a day."

"That seems like a lot."

"It's actually not. Apparently, most people are dehydrated and they don't even know it. So, they end up thinking that they're hungry when they're not."

I nod.

Ever since I've known her, Aurora has always been doing one health-related challenge or another.

Once she ate only cabbage soup for two weeks straight, the cayenne pepper, lemon water, and something else cleanse.

And, of course, there were the usual suspects, too.

South Beach Diet, Atkins, and who knows what else.

She has always been a beautiful woman with long legs and a trim figure. I'm not sure if any of these efforts were necessary, but she loves researching and trying out the latest diets and "approaches to healthy living," as she used to call them.

"Do you want something to eat?" I ask.

I guess if she's going to stay here, I have to play host.

"Um, sure, why not?" she says. "But let me see what you have. I'm actually in the middle of this thirty-day Whole30 challenge."

"What is that?"

"No processed foods of any kind. No sugar. No grains or legumes. No dairy. And I don't eat meat anymore."

"So, what does that leave?"

"Lots of healthy options. Leafy vegetables. Fruits, though I'm trying to limit them. Eggs. Fish."

"How's it going?"

She opens my refrigerator and scans the empty shelves for possible options.

"Well, actually. I can't remember what day I'm on, but the first week was really hard, but then I got used to it."

I pull out a bag of kale and a box of organic free range eggs. She nods in approval.

"What are you going to do after it's over?"

"Will definitely keep away from the processed foods as much as possible and the dairy."

"But you love cheese."

She shrugs. "Yeah, but I quit eating meat because of the way that animals are treated, and the dairy industry isn't that much better. They forcefully impregnate cows so they can give birth every year and then take away their babies."

Given all of her faults, Aurora has always had a very kind heart when it comes to animals.

"How are your horses?" I ask. She often posts pictures of herself riding around her ranch in Luxembourg.

"They're wonderful. I miss them terribly, of course. Oh, Elizabeth, my black mare, you would absolutely love her. She reminds me a lot of you."

I smile.

Some would take that as an offense being compared to a horse, but I know that from Aurora, it's one of the highest compliments she can offer.

"How's that?" I ask.

"Well, she was saved from a barn fire when I rescued her. She was sort of shut down for a while; it took her a long time to go out into the pasture with the others."

Wow, I did not expect this conversation to go *there* so quickly.

My jaw clenches up as I consider how to respond.

"I didn't mean that in a mocking way, Jackson. All I wanted to say is that I'm glad that you're... feeling better."

"I need a drink," I say, reaching for a bottle of whiskey from the liquor cabinet. "You want one?"

She narrows her eyes, thinking. "Um...yes...no. No, I'm going to be strong."

Aurora was never much of a drinker, so I'm a bit surprised that she has developed a problem.

"Are you...quitting?"

"No. It's a part of the thirty-day challenge. No alcohol."

That doesn't stop me from pouring myself a drink.

"But I'll join you," she says, reaching for one of the wine glasses. She pours her water into it.

When I'm about to take a sip, she stops me. "I wanted to say something first. Thank you so much for letting me stay here for a few days. Things are kind of tough right now and...I really appreciate you being my friend."

We clink our glasses.

I pour a bit of olive oil into the pan and heat it up.

I toss the kale into it first, covering it with a lid.

"This is going to be a very healthy meal," I say. "Probably the healthiest I've had in a long time."

"Well, you sure don't look it." Aurora smiles.

"What do you mean?"

"You look...really good. Fit...as always."

It sounds like she's hitting on me, but she's not.

She's just stating her opinion.

Being with someone who has known me for a very long time gives our interaction a natural ebb and flow.

We know what we mean without any confusion.

There's no second-guessing.

There's no misdirection.

On the other hand, there's also no surprise.

"So tell me what's been going on," I say, cracking the eggs into the pan.

I'm about to scramble them, but she stops me, wanting to keep hers sunny side up.

I don't have a preference and let them all go.

"You mean this?" She points to her black eye.

I wasn't exactly getting at that, but if she wants to start there, I won't object.

"Andrew and I have always had a bit of a volatile relationship."

"You don't say," I say sarcastically.

Andrew is Prince Andrew of Luxembourg, the nephew of the current Grand Duke Sebastian of Luxembourg, who is basically the King or the sovereign of the country.

They don't have any political powers, but just like the English monarchy they live in big mansions, do philanthropic work, and are fodder for local gossip magazines.

"You know you don't have to be with someone who puts his hands on you, right?" I say.

She laughs. "Oh, Jackson, I had forgotten how noble and innocent you are when it comes to marriage."

"Is that really such a crazy thing to say?"

She laughs, that kind of laugh that is a cover for something.

And then she shakes her head and looks away.

WHEN WE TALK...

*a*s we eat, Aurora opens up to me.

She has been married to Andrew for more than a few years now, and things were never that bad before.

They always had what she calls a "volatile" relationship, a code word for toxic, frantic, and out of control.

That's one of the reasons why we never worked.

I've never been one for loud, explosive fights that last all night and into the next day.

A part of her thrives on chaos. She seeks it out.

Before me, she was involved with a married man whose car she lit on fire, and soon after me she met Andrew.

They partied hard, played hard, and fought even harder.

"He never laid his hands on me before, until this year. We were always able to just...break stuff to get his frustrations out."

I nod.

"And he never cheated on me before either."

"He's cheating on you?"

"He denies it, of course, but I know that he is. He has known her for years. She's part of the Swedish monarchy, his second cousin removed or something like that. You know how they're all related. Well, there was this big party for New Year's and I saw them together. In the corner, alone. Kissing."

"What did you do?"

"I confronted him about it that night in our room. And he got violent. That was the first time he ever hit me."

Her eyes tear up, but she pushes her tears away.

"Why...why are you still with him?"

She shakes her head.

"I mean, you don't need the money. You don't need the title. You don't need him."

She shakes her head again. "I love him."

I take a deep breath, resisting the urge to roll my eyes.

Aurora and I have had our share of drama, but now I feel like our relationship has morphed into something resembling a brother and sister.

Very distant brother and sister.

She calls me when she's in crisis.

She talks.

I listen.

Give her some advice, which she doesn't follow.

And then I don't hear from her for a few months, maybe a year.

There was a time, a long time ago, when I did hate her the way divorced people are supposed to.

And I had good reason.

When she first left, she took off without saying a word.

One day she was there, being a mother, not a very present one but still.

And the next, she just vanished.

Later that evening, I got an email from her saying that she'd flown to London and wouldn't be back for a bit.

Lila, our daughter, was just a baby so she never really knew her, but when she got older she kept asking why she didn't have a mother and I didn't really have an answer for her.

Soon after partying her way around London, she

was hospitalized and placed on a mental hold at a psychiatric hospital.

Apparently, she was going through a major psychotic breakdown as a result of postpartum depression.

I felt like such a fool for not paying attention to any of the signs and my heart softened a bit when it came to her.

She married Andrew two days after our divorce was finalized and refused to see Lila again.

I wish she had, but she always maintained that it would've been too painful and her therapist had advised her to think of Lila as a child she gave up for adoption, to me.

It turned out to be a blessing in disguise. I didn't have to deal with custody issues.

I didn't have to worry about her spending time with Aurora or Andrew, for that matter. It was just the two of us all of her life and that was fine by me.

"So, tell me about you," Aurora says, finishing her food. "You leaving this house after all of this time...what brought about this change?"

Pictures of me driving around and attending formal events have been circulating on various social media accounts.

"Harley Burke."

"Ah, so...tell me everything," Aurora says excitedly.

After Lila's death, and my self-imposed seclusion, Aurora was one of the only people with whom I could talk about everything honestly.

A few months after the funeral, which she did not attend, she reached out to me and we just started texting each other.

The texts turned into an occasional phone call and then a weekly one.

While she wasn't there for me during our marriage and Lila's early years, she was there for me in the aftermath.

And she knew everything that I'd been going through.

"C'mon, tell me. She must be one hell of a girl."

I debate how much I should share and how much to leave out and eventually decide to just tell her the whole story.

She listens carefully and then says, "Wow, that sounds intense."

"So, what now?"

"Nothing." I shrug. "She's not answering my calls or texts. I went to her place a few times and she refused to come to the door. So...I think it's over."

Aurora shakes her head. "No, it's not."

I laugh. "How do you know that?"

"She'll come around. You didn't do anything that...egregious. I mean, you just asked a question."

"I know but that question represented the fact that I didn't believe her, at least in her mind."

Aurora shakes head again. "Just give her some time. It will all work out, trust me."

CHAPTER 36 - JACKSON

WHEN THERE'S A LIGHT AT THE END OF THE TUNNEL...

The following morning, Aurora comes in carrying bags with designer names on them while I'm eating breakfast.

"Agh, it feels so good to shop again! There's nothing like a bit of retail therapy to get you out of a slump."

She piles her bags on the dining room table and starts showing me her haul, completely ignoring my less than interested demeanor.

As she tells me about what she talked about with one saleswoman, she finally notices that I'm not exactly listening.

"Hello, Jackson, are you there?"

"No, sorry. I just have a lot on my mind," I say,

staring at my phone. "I just got a call from one of my lawyers. Apparently, Woodward is suing me."

"For what? Punching him?"

"Yeah, but you know it's a lot more than that. I bruised his ego so now he's going to make me pay."

"Sounds like he had it coming."

I shrug, that hardly matters.

"Well, I'm sure that your lawyers can reach some sort of settlement without this going to court."

That's probably true.

And given that it was only two punches, the settlement won't be that expensive.

The problem is that it's just another thing on top of all the other shit that has been going on.

I've mentioned some of the issues to Aurora before, but now I go into the nitty gritty details.

"So, how much money was Woodward going to invest originally?"

"About two million for a twenty percent share."

"And how much money do you need to keep Minetta operational for a few more months while you can find other sources of investment?"

"I don't know." I shrug.

"Give me a figure."

"Five hundred thousand? But I don't know if I can find other investors. Most of my money is gone so I can't exactly prop Minetta up with my personal funds for much longer. And on paper, due to all the expansions, it's bleeding money."

Aurora taps her fingers on the counter, lost in thought.

"You need a plan."

I shrug. "I'm all ears."

"One that doesn't include selling this house. Because you know that you're not going to get a good deal on it and whoever buys it will most likely separate it into luxury condos instead of keeping it as one historic mansion."

"I didn't know you were so into this place."

"Hell, yes. It's a part of New York history. And I helped you buy it originally if you remember."

"How could I forget? You don't waste an opportunity to remind me."

"Shh, let me think. So...Minetta is now operating entirely on advertising, correct? Articles and podcasts and videos get clicks and you sell advertising space based on those. Like google AdWords."

"Not exactly like Google AdWords, but yeah, you have the gist."

"So, what you are missing is revenue that comes

from somewhere else. Real products that you sell in exchange for money."

I roll my eyes. "You don't have to talk to me like I'm a five-year-old. I was mentioned in Forbes as one of the richest self-made people in the world."

"Yeah, yeah, whatever. And now you don't have shit."

"Okay, how about this?" She goes to her purse and takes out her checkbook. She writes a check and hands it to me.

It's for two million dollars.

"What are you doing? What is this?"

"This is the money that I'm going to invest in Minetta but under one condition. We're going to use it to figure out some way to create revenue that isn't based on advertising. You don't have to change any of your content; your content isn't the problem. People like it. Your problem is that you're not generating any money."

I DON'T ACCEPT the check right away, even though it's basically the only thing that will get me out of this horrendous mess.

Plus, I like her idea. I don't know why it hadn't

occurred to me before, selling related products is of course the obvious choice.

Most things are pretty easy and cheap to manufacture and given the size of our readership and social network, it is entirely possible that this company can be turned around and be made profitable again.

We spend the afternoon brainstorming.

I pull up a list of online magazines that we own and she helps me to come up with products, which fit the niche and the target audience of that content.

There are the usual suspects including mugs, notebooks, hats, and pens, but I push her to help me come up with something more relevant as well.

For example, a list of baby essentials for our two pregnancy blogs and a slew of kid products for our mom-related magazines.

These are just ideas, nothing is set in stone, and I plan to reach out to the content producers themselves and others in the organization to come up with and narrow the list of appropriate products that we will private label under the Minetta brand.

When the sun starts to set, I finally start to see a way out of this debacle.

"I think this is really going to work," Aurora says. "I mean, look at Costco and their Kirkland private label products. They stand side by side with all the other name brand products on their shelves and people buy them because they are Costco approved and usually a bit more affordable than the other guys."

I nod.

"It's just going to be a lot of work to find just the right products for the right audience, but I think it's going to work and make all the difference."

"You don't have to sell me on this anymore, Aurora. I'm on board."

She picks up her check from the table and hands it to me again.

"What kind of percentage are you looking for in return for this?"

"I thought that you'd never ask." She smiles.

"How about thirty?"

"Woodward was going to take twenty."

"Woodward didn't come up with a plan that will make you profitable within half a year."

I don't tell her this, but that's actually a lot better terms than I thought she would offer. I take the check and shake her hand.

CHAPTER 37 - HARLEY

WHEN I FINISH…

I finish the novel. I don't have a good title for it yet, but it's finished. Completely done with an idea for a sequel.

Perhaps, I'm getting ahead of myself.

Maybe I should just publish it first and then see if anyone even wants to read the second part of the story.

Or maybe I should just keep writing and not give a damn.

That sounds more like it.

I've spent a lot of time writing for other people and trying to figure out what the hell they want.

And now, this series of novels will be about me and what I want.

It has a rich guy, a poor girl, damaged histories,

and a whole host of obstacles as well as plenty of sexy bits.

It's lovely, based on the beginning of what Jackson and I were, but the story has since created a world of its own.

The characters no longer belong to me.

They are their own three-dimensional beings with their own hopes, desires, urges, and regrets.

Some writers think of themselves as God.

They create a whole world out of cloth and rule everyone in that story with an iron fist.

Some think of themselves as architects.

They map everything out.

They plan every twist and turn.

I'm not sure that I fall into either of those categories.

I see myself more as a mother.

I create a life, or lives, and then I watch them flower.

I throw some obstacles at them because what is life but an endless series of obstacles?

But what gives me encouragement and hope is how my characters overcome the odds.

I have re-read my novel a few times already, fixing a few mistakes each time.

I find a few proofreaders who are willing to read

my novel and correct the errors that I didn't catch at a reasonable price.

It should really go through two rounds, but I can't even really afford one.

So I choose the cheaper, but the friendlier one with more experience in indie romance, and she sends me a proof in two days.

There aren't that many mistakes, but there are still plenty. It was well worth the ninety bucks and while she had the document, I set out to learn how to make a cover.

I've taken one art class in college, but it taught me nothing about photoshop or graphic design.

But nowadays, there are so many different apps that help you put fancy words on images for social media purposes that I download a few and start playing around with them.

Through one of the social media groups for indie publishing, I learn about the various stock image websites where I can buy an image to use for my cover.

I debate whether I should go with a traditional shirtless man, which every romance reader knows means this book has something sexy inside, and an object cover with just a pair of cufflinks, a diamond necklace, or a pearl.

I've been doing my research and I've seen them popping up more and more.

Of course, there are the big names out there who rely entirely on object covers, but will it work for me?

I'm nobody. I just have one book.

I download a few images of both options.

Hot sexy abs vs a sparkling diamond.

Hot sexy abs vs a pair of cufflinks.

On one hand, it should be an easy choice.

But something draws me toward the objects.

They're a bit more visually interesting and not so outwardly sexual.

On the other hand, maybe that's a bad thing.

I don't want people to overlook my book because it doesn't have a hot sexy guy with a ridiculous six pack on the cover.

But before I can make a decision about this, I need a title.

A few possibilities run through my mind.

Alone.

Recluse.

Recluse Billionaire.

Saved by a Recluse Billionaire.

The last one isn't so much a title as a description

but it will definitely tell anyone who is interested what the book is about.

But do I want to be so direct?

Do I want to be so on the nose?

In reality, the book is so much more than that.

That's just the catalyst for what's to come.

Unable to make a decision, I put my laptop away and pace around the room.

I'd go for a walk, but it's already dark outside and the last time I was out I felt like someone was following me.

When that doesn't help, I flip on Netflix and lose myself in the latest binge. Somewhere around episode four, it comes to me.

Object cover, diamond. Recluse.

While the episode keeps running, I pick up my phone and pull up the image in the graphic design app.

I choose the book cover size, and then choose one style of typography for the title and another for my name.

They don't look that good together.

So I do it again.

And again.

And again.

Until I stumble on just the right combination.

And that's it.

Just like that...the book cover is done.

My heart skips a beat and I'm unable to contain my excitement.

I grab my computer and immediately log into Kindle Direct Publishing, where I already made an account.

I've looked at the layout of this website before and watched about five YouTube videos about how to upload the book to Amazon.

But in reality, the process is a lot smoother than I thought it would be. I upload the title, blurb, keywords, and the cover.

I have already converted the Word document to the right format for Kindle and all I have to do now is upload it here.

I set the price on the following page and then hover the mouse over the last button.

Publish.

There's a choice of publishing now or setting it up as a pre-order.

Without further delay, I press the publish button and the book is off.

Sitting back in the chair, I look at what I just did in awe.

No query letters.

No submissions of three chapters to literary agents who probably never even read the books that are submitted to them.

Yet, the book is on its way to get published.

Did this just happen?

CHAPTER 38 - HARLEY

WHEN I READ HIS LETTERS...

"So, are you ever going to talk to that boyfriend of yours and let him off the hook?" Julie asks.

At first, she was there for me, taking my side and listening to my complaints.

But the more Jackson tried to contact me, and the more times she had to turn him away from our doorstep, the harsher she became toward me.

"You really think I should forgive him?" I ask.

"You should at least talk to him. He didn't do anything that terrible for you to just ghost him."

"What about you and Logan?"

"What about us? I caught him cheating on me and I still talked to him. You need closure, Harley. I see you. Otherwise, you'll be stuck in this limbo forever."

My thoughts drift back toward Jackson.

I miss him.

I've tried to put him out of my mind.

I tried to forget him.

But no matter what, I didn't, he kept coming back to me.

Whenever I would close my eyes, I would see those high cheekbones.

His exquisite blue irises.

His thick lavish hair.

He is running his fingers down my arms.

He is kissing my neck.

He is tonguing my navel.

But it's not just his body that I find myself craving.

It's so much more than that.

He was there for me when I needed him most.

He took me home and he was there for the whole mess that turned out to be.

He held me while I cried, and most importantly he didn't push me away from him.

"What is it that he did exactly to deserve this?" she asks. "And don't go over the details, they don't matter. Tell me how he made you feel."

I think about that for a moment.

"I felt betrayed. He didn't believe me and it just... hurt me, you know, right in the heart."

"Now, I'm not trying to deny your feelings, but isn't it also possible that he was just trying to give you a way out?"

"Way out?"

"Maybe it was his way of telling you that you were in a safe place. That you could trust him. And if you did have a past, then that was okay with him."

"Yes...I guess it's possible."

"I don't know him, Harley. But you do. Put your pride away for just a moment and really think about this. Because the thing that you have with him, that doesn't come along too often. If ever. And you don't want to lose something over anything as stupid as a little bit of pride."

Her words run through my mind over and over until they force me into a realization that I'm not too keen on.

They say that time is the healer of all things, but in my case, it made me realize my own stupidity. I wasn't wrong to get mad.

I wasn't wrong to get upset or angry for what he did.

But throw away the special thing that we had,

this relationship that was just beginning to blossom...that was wrong.

Julie is right.

I have this tendency to shut people out.

Whenever anything gets difficult and I can't really deal with the confrontation, I just put up a guard.

It's as thick as plexiglass and nothing and no one can get through it.

I did that with my mom back when I found her cheating on my dad.

I didn't care why she was doing what she was doing.

I didn't want to hear any excuses or explanations.

She had lied to me and to my father and that was enough for me to write her out of my life.

Now, all of this time later, my father has managed to forgive her but I still haven't.

Am I making the same mistake with Jackson?

Am I being too harsh?

Too difficult?

He made one mistake and that was enough for me.

Enough for me to just say goodbye to him forever, without actually doing it.

I look through the letters that he had sent me.

There are a total of five of them.

All handwritten in perfect script, elegant, cursive, yet still readable.

They don't mention much about our fight except a brief apology in the beginning.

Instead, he writes about how much he loved Montana, especially the meadow in front of our house there.

He writes about the hawk circling overhead and the rabbit he had left carrots for. In another letter, he writes about walking with me in Central Park.

We haven't done it yet, so he just makes it up.

He talks about holding my hand and wrapping his arms around me when I got cold.

He talks about throwing a snowball at my back and me throwing one back at him right in the face.

I've never received letters like these before.

No, I haven't received any letters, but I've never read any like these before either. It's almost as if we are a couple from another time.

The last one is a bit different.

It describes how he felt the first time he saw me in my gown and the mask, using words like effervescent and breathtaking.

He doesn't mention anything that happened

there, but he does say that he has only one regret, that we didn't get to dance together that night.

Before signing the letter, he writes, "Will you dance with me?"

After re-reading all of the letters for what feels like the hundredth time, I place them all back in their respective envelopes.

And that's when I see it.

How could I have missed it?

It's a check.

For ten thousand dollars and it comes in the last letter.

The memo line reads "Advance for first novel."

My hand begins to tremble as I hold the check in my hand.

This money means everything.

It is the answer to all of my problems.

It would pay for the whole emergency visit, plus I'd have money left over.

I wouldn't worry about rent that much and I could really focus on this novel.

It's a lot of money, but I know that he's not trying to buy me. He wouldn't do that.

This money, just like those letters, are coming from a deeper place than that.

So, what do I do now?

CHAPTER 39 - JACKSON

WHEN THINGS DON'T GO AS PLANNED...

*I*t has been a few days since Aurora arrived and we have gotten into a bit of a rhythm.

She is gone most of the day, shopping and having lunch with friends she hasn't seen in nearly a year - the last time she was in New York.

While I work upstairs, making plans and going over ideas for our new area of focus. The idea to expand into selling products is genius.

I have no idea why it never occurred to me before. This way we are actually in control of our content.

We have money coming in from sources other than advertising, diversifying our business model and making it less risky.

Once Phillips and a few other people at the top start discussing this plan in more detail and I do a bit of my own research on how other companies have done this, I realize that it's actually everywhere.

Very few products are that original, meaning that they come with patents.

Most fall into this gray area, where it's all about branding and name recognition.

The key is, of course, to choose the right products for the right markets and audiences.

The process of doing this is progressing very smoothly and my team is excited about this avenue.

None of them have done this before, so I do a video conference meeting with a consultant in the area.

She goes over the details and gives us an action plan as to where to begin.

Within a few days, we have a number of must-have products chosen for almost every online magazine and content provider we have.

When I come downstairs, to take a break for lunch, my jaw nearly drops open.

I see Elliot Woodward kissing Aurora in the middle of my kitchen.

She's sitting on my island with her legs wrapped around his torso and his hands up her shirt.

"What the hell?"

"Hey, man, relax, you nearly gave me a heart attack."

Aurora jumps down to the floor, tucking her blouse back into her jeans.

"What are you doing here? What are you doing with him?"

"Look, you don't have to freak out, okay? Elliot and I just had some lunch and a bottle of wine, and we wanted to go somewhere more private."

I suddenly remember that she and Elliot dated briefly when she took off for London.

"Aurora, you're a guest here. You're not allowed to bring anyone over."

"Wait a second, now that's just a bit rude, don't you think?" Woodward says.

His words come out a bit slurred, but he quickly corrects himself.

"Why did you even come here? Didn't you file a lawsuit against me?" I ask him.

"That's what we were celebrating actually," Aurora says. "I met with Elliot to get him to drop that pesky lawsuit against you. And we got to talking and laughing…"

Her words trail off as if she forgets that she was speaking.

"No...well, yes...but once we started reminiscing, I couldn't say no anymore."

Woodward is still an asshole and I still have the urge to toss him out of my house.

But if he is willing to drop the lawsuit after one lunch with her, I don't want to do anything to jeopardize that.

Getting rid of unnecessary litigation at a time like this would go a long way toward making Minetta successful again.

"So... will you be dropping the lawsuit?" I ask Woodward.

He narrows his eyes and shrewdly stares at me.

No, there's no fucking way he's doing it.

He was just using that as bait to get Aurora a little drunk and vulnerable.

"Eh, what the hell." He puts out his hand. "Let's let bygones be bygones, huh?"

I clench my jaw, force a smile, and shake his hand.

"Sure, why not?"

AFTER WOODWARD LEAVES, Aurora turns to me and asks, "So, what do I get for doing this?"

I shake my head.

"What? Not even a thank you?"

"You're drunk."

"Still...I got him to cave. That's worth something, right."

"Thank you," I say through clenched teeth. "But you should be careful with him. He's a..."

"Egotistical sociopath? Narcissist? Yeah, I know. I mean, who the hell isn't, right?"

"There are good men out there, Aurora. You just never give them a chance."

"Oh, c'mon, I was just kidding."

"Well, I'm not."

"The thing is, Jackson, that I really, really like the bad ones. They're so much more fun."

I shake my head and walk away from her.

"Don't be mad." She walks up to me and throws her arms around me in a big bear hug.

She's definitely wasted.

She's not one to be particularly touchy-feely unless she's had a bit to drink.

I peel her hands away from me.

"I don't know why you're acting like this. I thought that you would be happy. I mean, he's going to drop the lawsuit. You owe me. Big!"

Our conversation is going in circles like a merry-go-round and I need to be the first one to step off if I want the ride to come to an end.

"I am happy that he's dropping the lawsuit, but I don't want him to do it at your expense."

She tilts her head to the side and rolls her eyes. "What?"

"Did you *not* see me enjoying myself? Did I not have my legs wrapped around that guy, ready to take this show to the bedroom?"

"Yes...you did."

"Good. So give me some credit. He's hot. He's fun. He's charming. And I wanted him. He wanted me. We are both consenting adults to do whatever the hell we want with each other."

I nod, at a loss for anything else to say.

She reaches out her hand and runs it through my hair.

She lets it linger there for a few moments before slowly running it down my shoulder.

I turn my head toward her and she continues to pet me.

"Still...there are nice guys out there, Aurora."

She lifts up my chin, bringing her face closer to mine. "I think you might be the only one left."

CHAPTER 40 - HARLEY

LIFE IS WHAT HAPPENS WHEN YOU'RE MAKING OTHER PLANS...

I get off the subway with a new-found pep in my step.

I am only two blocks away from his house and my body starts to tremble with excitement.

He's going to be surprised.

He's going to pull me inside and wrap his arms around me.

He's going to kiss me just like he did before, and everything is going to be okay again.

I take a deep breath as I walk up to his house.

His check for ten grand is tucked away safely inside my journal.

I want Jackson back, but I don't want his money.

I can do this on my own.

For a while there, I considered taking it with all

intentions of paying it back as if it were a loan, but I've had enough of indebtedness.

With Julie moving back in, I don't have to worry about her portion of the rent and I'm going to focus all of my efforts on living as frugally as possible, not eating out, saving every penny, and paying off my medical debt.

I take a deep breath and walk up to the house.

The curtains aren't drawn and from the street I can see him in the kitchen. I stand here watching him and smiling.

It's all going to be fixed after this.

I'm going to apologize, and it will be just like before.

And then...I see *her*.

She leans across the island and tucks his hair behind his ear.

She pauses for a moment to play with it, taking one curl and bringing it to the other side.

"Who are you?" I whisper.

My hands clam up and my toes turn to ice as all the blood inside of me seems to come to a stop.

But instead of pushing her away, Jackson seems to lean his head into her. I can't watch anymore.

I back away from the window and walk across the street in the opposite direction.

Thoughts swirl around in my head, examining the possibilities.

Maybe she was just a friend?

No, I've seen him around his friends and he never once acted so...sensual with them.

Maybe it was just a first date?

No.

You aren't that comfortable on a first date.

There's a tension in the air that was completely absent from the two of them.

No, that is someone that Jackson knows very well.

I try to pick up the pace, but my feet don't cooperate.

They entangle with one another and I almost trip.

"Harley."

There's so much blood rushing through my head that I don't hear his voice very well.

When I turn around, I look straight into the barrel of a gun.

It's long and deep, the color of charcoal.

He pulls the gun away from my eyes and points it at my chest.

"Get into the van," Parker says, gesturing to the white scuffed up van parked next to us.

I've seen enough crime shows to know that once you get into the car, it's pretty much over.

No one can find you.

"Get into the van, Harley, or I'll blow your head off right now."

"But then you'll have no one to stalk."

The words just escape my mouth before I can stop them.

I should be scared, but instead I'm angry.

At him, for pointing that gun at my face, but mostly at Jackson and the blonde.

He flicks the gun down for a moment and shoots.

Standing this close to a gunshot, it sounds nothing like a car backfiring. It's the sound of death.

He misses my foot by an inch and then points the gun at my chest again.

"I'm not fucking around."

I take a few steps toward the van.

"That's a good girl."

He opens the door and gestures for me to get in.

I follow his command and just as he's about to close it, I kick him really hard, knocking the gun out of his hand.

He jumps on top of me and closes the door behind us.

"Drive!"

He yells into my ear and we take off.

I try to punch him and kick him.

I get a few good ones in, but I still can't budge him.

Then he makes a fist and hits me in the jaw.

Everything turns to black.

THANK you for reading Tangled up in Pain!

I hope you are enjoying Harley and Jackson's story. Can't wait to find out what happens next?

One-click Tangled up in Lace now!

Our love isn't like everyone else's. I used to be a recluse, but no more.

She helped me fight my dark past.

Now, it's my turn to help her fight hers.

BUT SHE'S NOT HERE.

I have to find her and show her what I'm willing to do for her.

This is one thing I can't buy.

Am I willing to give up everything to have her?

One-click Tangled up in Lace now!

SIGN up for my **newsletter** to find out when I have new books!

You can also join my Facebook group, **Charlotte Byrd's Reader Club**, for exclusive giveaways and sneak peaks of future books.

I appreciate you sharing my books and telling your friends about them. Reviews help readers find my books! Please leave a review on your favorite site.

BLACK EDGE

*W*ant to read a "Decadent, delicious, & dangerously addictive!" romance you will not be able to put down? The entire series is out! **1-Click Black Edge NOW!**

I don't belong here.

I'm in way over my head. But I have debts to pay.

They call my name. The spotlight is on. The auction starts.

Mr. Black is the highest bidder. He's dark, rich, and powerful. He likes to play games.

The only rule is there are no rules.

But it's just one night. **What's the worst that can happen?**

1-Click BLACK EDGE Now!

* * *

START READING BLACK EDGE ON THE NEXT PAGE!

CHAPTER 1- ELLIE

WHEN THE INVITATION ARRIVES...

"*H*ere it is! Here it is!" my roommate Caroline yells at the top of her lungs as she runs into my room.

We were friends all through Yale and we moved to New York together after graduation.

Even though I've known Caroline for what feels like a million years, I am still shocked by the exuberance of her voice. It's quite loud given the smallness of her body.

Caroline is one of those super skinny girls who can eat pretty much anything without gaining a pound.

Unfortunately, I am not that talented. In fact, my body seems to have the opposite gift. I can eat nothing but vegetables for a week straight, eat one slice of pizza, and gain a pound.

"What is it?" I ask, forcing myself to sit up.

It's noon and I'm still in bed.

My mother thinks I'm depressed and wants me to see her shrink.

She might be right, but I can't fathom the strength.

"The invitation!" Caroline says jumping in bed next to me.

I stare at her blankly.

And then suddenly it hits me.

This must be *the* invitation.

"You mean...it's..."

"Yes!" she screams and hugs me with excitement.

"Oh my God!" She gasps for air and pulls away from me almost as quickly.

"Hey, you know I didn't brush my teeth yet," I say turning my face away from hers.

"Well, what are you waiting for? Go brush them," she instructs.

Begrudgingly, I make my way to the bathroom.

We have been waiting for this invitation for some time now.

And by we, I mean Caroline.

I've just been playing along, pretending to care, not really expecting it to show up.

Without being able to contain her excitement, Caroline bursts through the door when my mouth is still full of toothpaste.

She's jumping up and down, holding a box in her hand.

"Wait, what's that?" I mumble and wash my mouth out with water.

"This is it!" Caroline screeches and pulls me into the living room before I have a chance to wipe my mouth with a towel.

"But it's a box," I say staring at her.

"Okay, okay," Caroline takes a couple of deep yoga breaths, exhaling loudly.

She puts the box carefully on our dining room table. There's no address on it.

It looks something like a fancy gift box with a big monogrammed C in the middle.

Is the C for Caroline?

"Is this how it came? There's no address on it?" I ask.

"It was hand-delivered," Caroline whispers.

I hold my breath as she carefully removes the top part, revealing the satin and silk covered wood box inside.

The top of it is gold plated with whimsical twirls all around the edges, and the mirrored area is engraved with her full name.

Caroline Elizabeth Kennedy Spruce.

Underneath her name is a date, one week in the future. 8 PM.

We stare at it for a few moments until Caroline reaches for the elegant knob to open the box.

Inside, Caroline finds a custom monogram made of foil in gold on silk emblazoned on the inside of the flap cover.

There's also a folio covered in silk. Caroline carefully opens the folio and finds another foil monogram and the invitation.

The inside invitation is one layer, shimmer white, with gold writing.

"Is this for real? How many layers of invitation are there?" I ask.

But the presentation is definitely doing its job. We are both duly impressed.

"There's another knob," I say, pointing to the knob in front of the box.

I'm not sure how we had missed it before.

Caroline carefully pulls on this knob, revealing a drawer that holds the inserts (a card with directions and a response card).

"Oh my God, I can't go to this alone," Caroline mumbles, turning to me.

I stare blankly at her.

Getting invited to this party has been her dream ever since she found out about it from someone in the Cicada 17, a super-secret society at Yale.

"Look, here, it says that I can bring a friend," she yells out even though I'm standing right next to her.

"It probably says a date. A plus one?" I say.

"No, a friend. Girl preferred," Caroline reads off the invitation card.

That part of the invitation is in very small ink, as if someone made the person stick it on, without their express permission.

"I don't want to crash," I say.

Frankly, I don't really want to go.

These kind of upper-class events always make me feel a little bit uncomfortable.

"Hey, aren't you supposed to be at work?" I ask.

"Eh, I took a day off," Caroline says waving her arm. "I knew that the invitation would come today and I just couldn't deal with work. You know how it is."

I nod. Sort of.

Caroline and I seem like we come from the same world.

We both graduated from private school, we both went to Yale, and our parents belong to the same exclusive country club in Greenwich, Connecticut.

But we're not really that alike.

Caroline's family has had money for many generations going back to the railroads.

My parents were an average middle class family from Connecticut.

They were both teachers and our idea of summering was renting a 1-bedroom bungalow near Clearwater, FL for a week.

But then my parents got divorced when I was 8, and my mother started tutoring kids to make extra money.

The pay was the best in Greenwich, where parents paid more than $100 an hour.

And that's how she met, Mitch Willoughby, my stepfather.

He was a widower with a five-year old daughter who was not doing well after her mom's untimely death.

Even though Mom didn't usually tutor anyone younger than 12, she agreed to take a meeting with Mitch and his daughter because $200 an hour was too much to turn down.

Three months later, they were in love and six

months later, he asked her to marry him on top of the Eiffel Tower.

They got married, when I was 11, in a huge 450-person ceremony in Nantucket.

So even though Caroline and I run in the same circles, we're not really from the same circle.

It has nothing to do with her, she's totally accepting, it's me.

I don't always feel like I belong.

Caroline majored in art-history at Yale, and she now works at an exclusive contemporary art gallery in Soho.

It's chic and tiny, featuring only 3 pieces of art at a time.

Ash, the owner - I'm not sure if that's her first or last name - mainly keeps the space as a showcase. What the gallery really specializes in is going to wealthy people's homes and choosing their art for them.

They're basically interior designers, but only for art.

None of the pieces sell for anything less than $200 grand, but Caroline's take home salary is about $21,000.

Clearly, not enough to pay for our 2 bedroom apartment in Chelsea.

Her parents cover her part of the rent and pay all of her other expenses.

Mine do too, of course.

Well, Mitch does.

I only make about $27,000 at my writer's assistant job and that's obviously not covering my half of our $6,000 per month apartment.

So, what's the difference between me and Caroline?

I guess the only difference is that I feel bad about taking the money.

I have a $150,000 school loan from Yale that I don't want Mitch to pay for.

It's my loan and I'm going to pay for it myself, dammit.

Plus, unlike Caroline, I know that real people don't really live like this.

Real people like my dad, who is being pressured to sell the house for more than a million dollars that he and my mom bought back in the late 80's (the neighborhood has gone up in price and teachers now have to make way for tech entrepreneurs and real estate moguls).

"How can you just not go to work like that? Didn't you use all of your sick days flying to Costa Rica last month?" I ask.

"Eh, who cares? Ash totally understands. Besides, she totally owes me. If it weren't for me, she would've never closed that geek millionaire who had the hots for me and ended up buying close to a million dollars' worth of art for his new mansion."

Caroline does have a way with men.

She's fun and outgoing and perky.

The trick, she once told me, is to figure out exactly what the guy wants to hear.

Because a geek millionaire, as she calls anyone who has made money in tech, does not want to hear the same thing that a football player wants to hear.

And neither of them want to hear what a trust fund playboy wants to hear.

But Caroline isn't a gold digger.

Not at all.

Her family owns half the East Coast.

And when it comes to men, she just likes to have fun.

I look at the time.

It's my day off, but that doesn't mean that I want to spend it in bed in my pajamas, listening to Caroline obsessing over what she's going to wear.

No, today, is my day to actually get some writing done.

I'm going to Starbucks, getting a table in the

back, near the bathroom, and am actually going to finish this short story that I've been working on for a month.

Or maybe start a new one.

I go to my room and start getting dressed.

I have to wear something comfortable, but something that's not exactly work clothes.

I hate how all of my clothes have suddenly become work clothes. It's like they've been tainted.

They remind me of work and I can't wear them out anymore on any other occasion. I'm not a big fan of my work, if you can't tell.

Caroline follows me into my room and plops down on my bed.

I take off my pajamas and pull on a pair of leggings.

Ever since these have become the trend, I find myself struggling to force myself into a pair of jeans.

They're just so comfortable!

"Okay, I've come to a decision," Caroline says. "You *have* to come with me!"

"Oh, I have to come with you?" I ask, incredulously. "Yeah, no, I don't think so."

"Oh c'mon! Please! Pretty please! It will be so much fun!"

"Actually, you can't make any of those promises.

You have no idea what it will be," I say, putting on a long sleeve shirt and a sweater with a zipper in the front.

Layers are important during this time of year.

The leaves are changing colors, winds are picking up, and you never know if it's going to be one of those gorgeous warm, crisp New York days they like to feature in all those romantic comedies or a soggy, overcast dreary day that only shows up in one scene at the end when the two main characters fight or break up (but before they get back together again).

"Okay, yes, I see your point," Caroline says, sitting up and crossing her legs. "But here is what we *do* know. We do know that it's going to be amazing. I mean, look at the invitation. It's a freakin' box with engravings and everything!"

Usually, Caroline is much more eloquent and better at expressing herself.

"Okay, yes, the invitation is impressive," I admit.

"And as you know, the invitation is everything. I mean, it really sets the mood for the party. The event! And not just the mood. It establishes a certain expectation. And this box..."

"Yes, the invitation definitely sets up a certain expectation," I agree.

"So?"

"So?" I ask her back.

"Don't you want to find out what that expectation is?"

"No." I shake my head categorically.

"Okay. So what else do we know?" Caroline asks rhetorically as I pack away my Mac into my bag.

"I have to go, Caroline," I say.

"No, listen. The yacht. Of course, the yacht. How could I bury the lead like that?" She jumps up and down with excitement again.

"We also know that it's going to be this super exclusive event on a *yacht*! And not just some small 100 footer, but a *mega*-yacht."

I stare at her blankly, pretending to not be impressed.

When Caroline first found out about this party, through her ex-boyfriend, we spent days trying to figure out what made this event so special.

But given that neither of us have been on a yacht before, at least not a mega-yacht – we couldn't quite get it.

"You know the yacht is going to be amazing!"

"Yes, of course," I give in. "But that's why I'm sure that you're going to have a wonderful time by yourself. I have to go."

I grab my keys and toss them into the bag.

"Ellie," Caroline says.

The tone of her voice suddenly gets very serious, to match the grave expression on her face.

"Ellie, please. I don't think I can go by myself."

CHAPTER 2 - ELLIE

WHEN YOU HAVE COFFEE WITH A GUY YOU CAN'T HAVE...

*a*nd that's pretty much how I was roped into going.

You don't know Caroline, but if you did, the first thing you'd find out is that she is not one to take things seriously.

Nothing fazes her.

Nothing worries her.

Sometimes she is the most enlightened person on earth, other times she's the densest.

Most of the time, I'm jealous of the fact that she simply lives life in the present.

"So, you're going?" my friend Tom asks.

He brought me my pumpkin spice latte, the first one of the season!

I close my eyes and inhale it's sweet aroma before taking the first sip.

But even before its wonderful taste of cinnamon and nutmeg runs down my throat, Tom is already criticizing my decision.

"I can't believe you're actually going," he says.

"Oh my God, now I know it's officially fall," I change the subject.

"Was there actually such a thing as autumn before the pumpkin spice latte? I mean, I remember that we had falling leaves, changing colors, all that jazz, but without this...it's like Christmas without a Christmas tree."

"Ellie, it's a day after Labor Day," Tom rolls his eyes. "It's not fall yet."

I take another sip. "Oh yes, I do believe it is."

"Stop changing the subject," Tom takes a sip of his plain black coffee.

How he doesn't get bored with that thing, I'll never know.

But that's the thing about Tom.

He's reliable.

Always on time, never late.

It's nice. That's what I have always liked about him.

He's basically the opposite of Caroline in every way.

And that's what makes seeing him like this, as only a friend, so hard.

"Why are you going there? Can't Caroline go by herself?" Tom asks, looking straight into my eyes.

His hair has this annoying tendency of falling into his face just as he's making a point – as a way of accentuating it.

It's actually quite vexing especially given how irresistible it makes him look.

His eyes twinkle under the low light in the back of the Starbucks.

"I'm going as her plus one," I announce.

I make my voice extra perky on purpose.

So that it portrays excitement, rather than apprehensiveness, which is actually how I'm feeling over the whole thing.

"She's making you go as her plus one," Tom announces as a matter a fact. He knows me too well.

"I just don't get it, Ellie. I mean, why bother? It's a super yacht filled with filthy rich people. I mean, how fun can that party be?"

"Jealous much?" I ask.

"I'm not jealous at all!" He jumps back in his seat. "If that's what you think…"

He lets his words trail off and suddenly the conversation takes on a more serious mood.

"You don't have to worry, I'm not going to miss your engagement party," I say quietly. It's the weekend after I get back."

He shakes his head and insists that that's not what he's worried about.

"I just don't get it Ellie," he says.

You don't get it?

You don't get why I'm going?

I've had feelings for you for, what, two years now?

But the time was never right.

At first, I was with my boyfriend and the night of our breakup, you decided to kiss me.

You totally caught me off guard.

And after that long painful breakup, I wasn't ready for a relationship.

And you, my best friend, you weren't really a rebound contender.

And then, just as I was about to tell you how I felt, you spend the night with Carrie.

Beautiful, wealthy, witty Carrie. Carrie Warrenhouse, the current editor of BuzzPost, the online magazine where we both work, and the daughter of Edward Warrenhouse, the owner of BuzzPost.

Oh yeah, and on top of all that, you also started seeing her and then asked her to marry you.

And now you two are getting married on Valentine's Day.

And I'm really happy for you.

Really.

Truly.

The only problem is that I'm also in love with you.

And now, I don't know what the hell to do with all of this except get away from New York.

Even if it's just for a few days.

But of course, I can't say any of these things.

Especially the last part.

"This hasn't been the best summer," I say after a few moments. "And I just want to do something fun. Get out of town. Go to a party. Because that's all this is, a party."

"That's not what I heard," Tom says.

"What do you mean?"

"Ever since you told me you were going, I started looking into this event.

And the rumor is that it's not what it is."

I shake my head, roll my eyes.

"What? You don't believe me?" Tom asks incredulously.

I shake my head.

"Okay, what? What did you hear?"

"It's basically like a Playboy Mansion party on steroids. It's totally out of control. Like one big orgy."

"And you would know what a Playboy Mansion party is like," I joke.

"I'm being serious, Ellie. I'm not sure this is a good place for you. I mean, you're not Caroline."

"And what the hell does that mean?" I ask.

Now, I'm actually insulted.

At first, I was just listening because I thought he was being protective.

But now...

"What you don't think I'm fun enough? You don't think I like to have a good time?" I ask.

"That's not what I meant," Tom backtracks. I start to gather my stuff. "What are you doing?"

"No, you know what," I stop packing up my stuff. "I'm not leaving. You're leaving."

"Why?"

"Because I came here to write. I have work to do. I staked out this table and I'm not leaving until I have something written. I thought you wanted to have coffee with me. I thought we were friends. I didn't realize that you came here to chastise me about my decisions."

"That's not what I'm doing," Tom says, without getting out of his chair.

"You have to leave Tom. I want you to leave."

"I just don't understand what happened to us," he says getting up, reluctantly.

I stare at him as if he has lost his mind.

"You have no right to tell me what I can or can't do. You don't even have the right to tell your fiancée. Unless you don't want her to stay your fiancée for long."

"I'm not trying to tell you what to do, Ellie. I'm just worried. This super exclusive party on some mega-yacht, that's not you. That's not us."

"Not us? You've got to be kidding," I shake my head. "You graduated from Princeton, Tom. Your father is an attorney at one of the most prestigious law-firms in Boston. He has argued cases before the Supreme Court. You're going to marry the heir to the Warrenhouse fortune. I'm so sick and tired of your working class hero attitude, I can't even tell you. Now, are you going to leave or should I?"

The disappointment that I saw in Tom's eyes hurt me to my very soul.

But he had hurt me.

His engagement came completely out of left field.

I had asked him to give me some time after my breakup and after waiting for only two months, he started dating Carrie.

And then they moved in together. And then he asked her to marry him.

And throughout all that, he just sort of pretended that we were still friends.

Just like none of this ever happened.

I open my computer and stare at the half written story before me.

Earlier today, before Caroline, before Tom, I had all of these ideas.

I just couldn't wait to get started.

But now...I doubted that I could even spell my name right.

Staring at a non-moving blinker never fuels the writing juices.

I close my computer and look around the place.

All around me, people are laughing and talking.

Leggings and Uggs are back in season – even though the days are still warm and crispy.

It hasn't rained in close to a week and everyone's

good mood seems to be energized by the bright rays of the afternoon sun.

Last spring, I was certain that Tom and I would get together over the summer and I would spend the fall falling in love with my best friend.

And now?

Now, he's engaged to someone else.

Not just someone else – my boss!

And we just had a fight over some stupid party that I don't even really want to go to.

He's right, of course.

It's not my style.

My family might have money, but that's not the world in which I'm comfortable.

I'm always standing on the sidelines and it's not going to be any different at this party.

But if I don't go now, after this, that means that I'm listening to him.

And he has no right to tell me what to do.

So, I have to go.

How did everything get so messed up?

CHAPTER 3 - ELLIE

WHEN YOU GO SHOPPING FOR THE
PARTY OF A LIFETIME...

"What the hell are you still doing hanging out with that asshole?" Caroline asks dismissively.

We are in Elle's, a small boutique in Soho, where you can shop by appointment only.

I didn't even know these places existed until Caroline introduced me to the concept.

Caroline is not a fan of Tom.

They never got along, not since he called her an East Side snob at our junior year Christmas party at Yale and she called him a middle class poseur.

Neither insult was very creative, but their insults got better over the years as their hatred for each other grew.

You know how in the movies, two characters who

hate each other in the beginning always end up
falling in love by the end?

Well, for a while, I actually thought that would
happen to them.

If not fall in love, at least hook up. But no, they
stayed steadfast in their hatred.

"That guy is such a tool. I mean, who the hell is
he to tell you what to do anyway? It's not like you're
his girlfriend," Caroline says placing a silver beaded
bandage dress to her body and extending her right
leg in front.

Caroline is definitely a knock out.

She's 5'10", 125 pounds with legs that go up to
her chin.

In fact, from far away, she seems to be all blonde
hair and legs and nothing else.

"I think he was just concerned, given all the stuff
that is out there about this party."

"Okay, first of all, you have to stop calling it
a party."

"Why? What is it?"

"It's not a party. It's like calling a wedding a party.
Is it a party? Yes. But is it bigger than that."

"I had no idea that you were so sensitive to
language. Fine. What do you want me to call it?'

"An experience," she announces, completely seriously.

"Are you kidding me? No way. There's no way I'm going to call it an experience."

We browse in silence for a few moments.

Some of the dresses and tops and shoes are pretty, some aren't.

I'm the first to admit that I do not have the vocabulary or knowledge to appreciate a place like this.

Now, Caroline on the other hand...

"Oh my God, I'm just in love with all these one of a kind pieces you have here," she says to the woman upfront who immediately starts to beam with pride.

"That's what we're going for."

"These statement bags and the detailing on these booties – agh! To die for, right?" Caroline says and they both turn to me.

"Yeah, totally," I agree blindly.

"And these high-end core pieces, I could just wear this every day!" Caroline pulls up a rather structured cream colored short sleeve shirt with a tassel hem and a boxy fit.

I'm not sure what makes that shirt a so-called core piece, but I go with the flow.

I'm out of my element and I know it.

"Okay, so what are we supposed to wear to this *experience* if we don't even know what's going to be going on there."

"I'm not exactly sure but definitely not jeans and t-shirts," Caroline says referring to my staple outfit. "But the invitation also said not to worry. They have all the necessities if we forget something."

As I continue to aimlessly browse, my mind starts to wander.

And goes back to Tom.

I met Tom at the Harvard-Yale game.

He was my roommate's boyfriend's high school best friend and he came up for the weekend to visit him.

We became friends immediately.

One smile from him, even on Skype, made all of my worries disappear.

He just sort of got me, the way no one really did.

After graduation, we applied to work a million different online magazines and news outlets, but BuzzPost was the one place that took both of us.

We didn't exactly plan to end up at the same place, but it was a nice coincidence.

He even asked if I wanted to be his roommate – but I had already agreed to room with Caroline.

He ended up in this crappy fourth floor walkup

in Hell's Kitchen – one of the only buildings that they haven't gentrified yet.

So, the rent was still somewhat affordable. Like I said, Tom likes to think of himself as a working class hero even though his upbringing is far from it.

Whenever he came over to our place, he always made fun of how expensive the place was, but it was always in good fun.

At least, it felt like it at the time.

Now?

I'm not so sure anymore.

"Do you think that Tom is really going to get married?" I ask Caroline while we're changing.

She swings my curtain open in front of the whole store.

I'm topless, but luckily I'm facing away from her and the assistant is buried in her phone.

"What are you doing?" I shriek and pull the curtain closed.

"What are you thinking?" she demands.

I manage to grab a shirt and cover myself before Caroline pulls the curtain open again.

She is standing before me in only a bra and a matching pair of panties – completely confident and unapologetic.

I think she's my spirit animal.

"Who cares about Tom?" Caroline demands.

"I do," I say meekly.

"Well, you shouldn't. He's a dick. You are way too good for him. I don't even understand what you see in him."

"He's my friend," I say as if that explains everything.

Caroline knows how long I've been in love with Tom.

She knows everything.

At times, I wish I hadn't been so open.

But other times, it's nice to have someone to talk to.

Even if she isn't exactly understanding.

"You can't just go around pining for him, Ellie. You can do so much better than him. You were with your ex and he just hung around waiting and waiting. Never telling you how he felt. Never making any grand gestures."

Caroline is big on gestures.

The grander the better.

She watches a lot of movies and she demands them of her dates.

And the funny thing is that you often get exactly what you ask from the world.

"I don't care about that," I say. "We were in the wrong place for each other.

I was with someone and then I wasn't ready to jump into another relationship right away.

And then...he and Carrie got together."

"There's no such thing as not the right time. Life is what you make it, Ellie. You're in control of your life. And I hate the fact that you're acting like you're not the main character in your own movie."

"I don't even know what you're talking about," I say.

"All I'm saying is that you deserve someone who tells you how he feels. Someone who isn't afraid of rejection. Someone who isn't afraid to put it all out there."

"Maybe that's who you want," I say.

"And that's not who you want?" Caroline says taking a step back away from me.

I think about it for a moment.

"Well, no I wouldn't say that. It is who I want," I finally say. "But I had a boyfriend then. And Tom and I were friends. So I couldn't expect him to—"

"You couldn't expect him to put it all out there? Tell you how he feels and take the risk of getting hurt?" Caroline cuts me off.

I hate to admit it, but that's exactly what I want.

That's exactly what I wanted from him
back then.

I didn't want him to just hang around being my
friend, making me question my feelings for him.

And if he had done that, if he had told me how
he felt about me earlier, before my awful breakup,
then I would've jumped in.

I would've broken up with my ex immediately to
be with him.

"So, is that what I should do now? Now that
things are sort of reversed?" I ask.

"What do you mean?"

"I mean, now that he's the one in the
relationship. Should I just put it all out there? Tell
him how I feel. Leave it all on the table, so to speak."

Caroline takes a moment to think about this.

I appreciate it because I know how little she
thinks of him.

"Because I don't know if I can," I add quietly.

"Maybe that's your answer right there," Caroline
finally says. "If you did want him, really want him to
be yours, then you wouldn't be able to not to. You'd
have to tell him."

I go back into my dressing room and pull the
curtain closed.

I look at myself in the mirror.

The pale girl with green eyes and long dark hair is a coward.

She is afraid of life.

Afraid to really live.

Would this ever change?

CHAPTER 4 - ELLIE

WHEN YOU DECIDE TO LIVE
YOUR LIFE…

"*A*re you ready?" Caroline bursts into my room. "Our cab is downstairs."

No, I'm not ready.

Not at all.

But I'm going.

I take one last look in the mirror and grab my suitcase.

As the cab driver loads our bags into the trunk, Caroline takes my hand, giddy with excitement.

Excited is not how I would describe my state of being.

More like reluctant.

And terrified.

When I get into the cab, my stomach drops and I feel like I'm going to throw up.

But then the feeling passes.

"I can't believe this is actually happening," I say.

"I know, right? I'm so happy you're doing this with me, Ellie. I mean, really. I don't know if I could go by myself."

After ten minutes of meandering through the convoluted streets of lower Manhattan, the cab drops us off in front of a nondescript office building.

"Is the party here?" I ask.

Caroline shakes her head with a little smile on her face.

She knows something I don't know.

I can tell by that mischievous look on her face.

"What's going on?" I ask.

But she doesn't give in.

Instead, she just nudges me inside toward the security guard at the front desk.

She hands him a card, he nods, and shows us to the elevator.

"Top floor," he says.

When we reach the top floor, the elevator doors swing open on the roof and a strong gust of wind knocks into me.

Out of the corner of my eye, I see it.

The helicopter.

The blades are already going.

A man approaches us and takes our bags.

"What are we doing here?" I yell on top of my lungs.

But Caroline doesn't hear me.

I follow her inside the helicopter, ducking my head to make sure that I get in all in one piece.

A few minutes later, we take off.

We fly high above Manhattan, maneuvering past the buildings as if we're birds.

I've never been in a helicopter before and, a part of me, wishes that I'd had some time to process this beforehand.

"I didn't tell you because I thought you would freak," Caroline says into her headset.

She knows me too well.

She pulls out her phone and we pose for a few selfies.

"It's beautiful up here," I say looking out the window.

In the afternoon sun, the Manhattan skyline is breathtaking.

The yellowish red glow bounces off the glass buildings and shimmers in the twilight.

I don't know where we are going, but for the first time in a long time, I don't care.

I stay in the moment and enjoy it for everything it's worth.

Quickly the skyscrapers and the endless parade of bridges disappear and all that remains below us is the glistening of the deep blue sea.

And then suddenly, somewhere in the distance I see it.

The yacht.

At first, it appears as barely a speck on the horizon.

But as we fly closer, it grows in size.

By the time we land, it seems to be the size of its own island.

* * *

A TALL, beautiful woman waves to us as we get off the helicopter.

She's holding a plate with glasses of champagne and nods to a man in a tuxedo next to her to take our bags.

"Wow, that was quite an entrance," Caroline says to me.

"Mr. Black knows how to welcome his guests,"

292

the woman says. "My name is Lizbeth and I am here to serve you."

Lizbeth shows us around the yacht and to our stateroom.

"There will be cocktails right outside when you're ready," Lizbeth said before leaving us alone.

As soon as she left, we grabbed hands and let out a big yelp.

"Oh my God! Can you believe this place?" Caroline asks.

"No, it's amazing," I say, running over to the balcony. The blueness of the ocean stretched out as far as the eye could see.

"Are you going to change for cocktails?" Caroline asks, sitting down at the vanity. "The helicopter did a number on my hair."

We both crack up laughing.

Neither of us have ever been on a helicopter before – let alone a boat this big.

I decide against a change of clothes – my Nordstrom leggings and polka dot blouse should do just fine for cocktail hour.

But I do slip off my pair of flats and put on a nice pair of pumps, to dress up the outfit a little bit.

While Caroline changes into her short black

dress, I brush the tangles out of my hair and reapply my lipstick.

"Ready?" Caroline asks.

Can't wait to read more? **One-Click BLACK EDGE Now!**

ABOUT CHARLOTTE BYRD

*C*harlotte Byrd is the bestselling author of many contemporary romance novels. She lives in Southern California with her husband, son, and a crazy toy Australian Shepherd. She loves books, hot weather and crystal blue waters.

Write her here:

charlotte@charlotte-byrd.com

Check out her books here:

www.charlotte-byrd.com

Connect with her here:

www.facebook.com/charlottebyrdbooks

Instagram: @charlottebyrdbooks

Twitter: @ByrdAuthor

Facebook Group: Charlotte Byrd's Reader Club

Newsletter

CPSIA information can be obtained
at www.ICGtesting.com
Printed in the USA
LVHW091321120919
630857LV00001B/157/P